Charlie

USA TODAY & WSJ BESTSELLING AUTHOR

SIOBHAN DAVIS

This paperback edition © February 2024

ISBN-13: 978-1-959285-29-8

Edited by Kelly Hartigan (XterraWeb) editing.xterraweb.com
Cover design by Shannon Passmore of Shanoff Designs
Cover imagery © bigstockphoto.com and stock.adobe.com
Crests & logos designed by Robin Harper of Wicked by Design
Formatted by Ciara Turley using Vellum

BOOK DESCRIPTION

Demi

Dropping out of college senior year was never part of my plan. But Dad needs me, and I'd move mountains for the only parent I've ever known—even working for the company that fired him.

My boss, Charlie, is determined to make my life a living hell, availing of every opportunity to undermine my confidence, to humiliate and threaten me.

Sleeping with him the night of his wedding might have something to do with his attitude.

Or the fact I'm the spitting image of the woman he really wants.

If our financial situation wasn't so dire, I'd tell Charlie to stick his job up his delectable butt.

But I'm trapped, and things are only getting worse. Because the more layers I uncover, the more I realize he is nothing I expected and everything I crave.

Charlie

If there was a manual for all the ways a person could mess up his life, it'd have my name written on it.

I can't undo the things I've done, no matter how badly I want to, and every day is a constant reminder of my epic failure.

Especially *her*.

It's as if Demi has been put on this earth to punish me. To inflict more torture and pain. Because every second I'm around her, she makes me feel things I don't want to feel.

So, I lash out. Doing my best to push her away.

Until I realize she's everything I never knew I needed, and the fight becomes a new battle—one to win her heart.

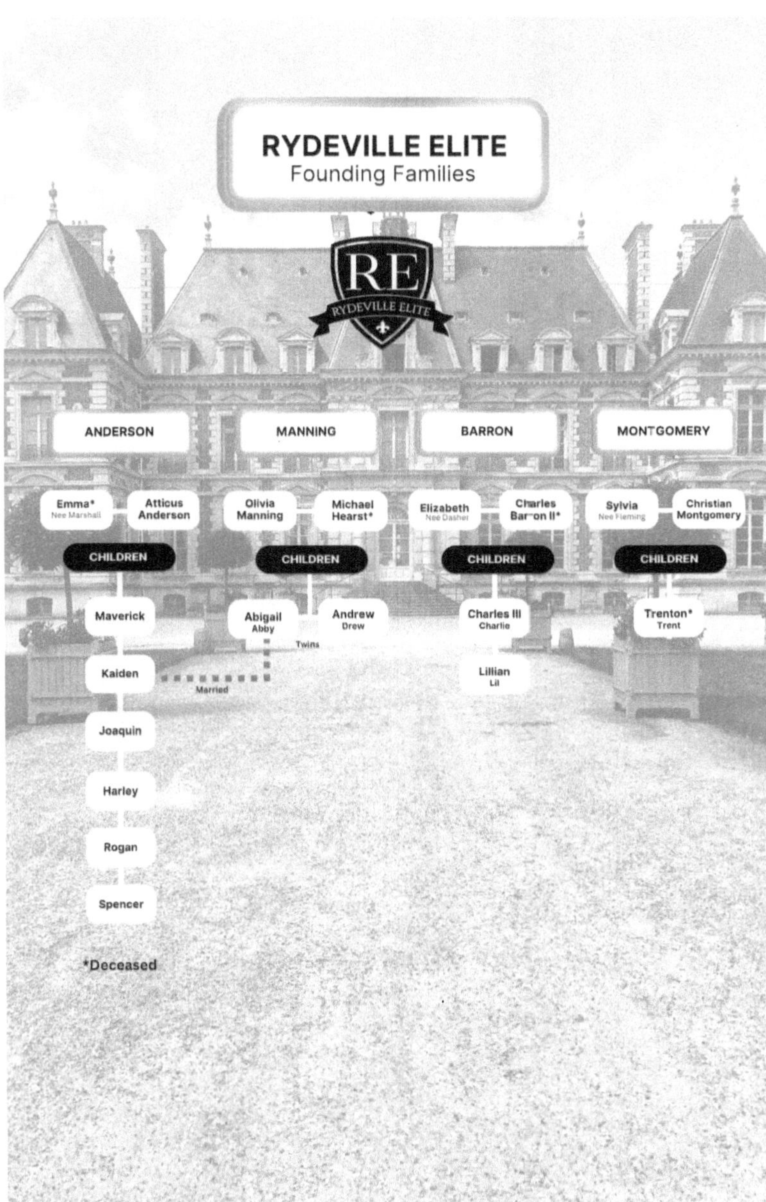

RYDEVILLE ELITE
Founding Families
RE
RYDEVILLE ELITE
ANDERSON
MANNING
BARRON
MONTGOMERY
Emma*
Nee Marshall
Atticus Anderson
Olivia Manning
Michael Hearst*
Elizabeth
Nee Dasher
Charles Barron II*
Sylvia
Nee Fleming
Christian Montgomery
CHILDREN
CHILDREN
CHILDREN
CHILDREN
Maverick
Abigail
Abby
Andrew
Drew
Charles III
Charlie
Trenton*
Trent
Twins
Kaiden
Lillian
Lil
Married
Joaquin
Harley
Rogan
Spencer
*Deceased

Charlie

Prologue
Demi – Christmas Night

Rhythmic beats reverberate through the speakers, mingling with the sounds of boisterous laughter and raucous chatter as I glance at my watch and sigh. I grab hold of Xena's arm, admiring her colorful ink, as I pull her down closer. "I've got to go," I shout in her ear, a necessity in this noisy room if I want to be heard.

She loops her arm in mine. "Aw, not yet, babe. The night's still young." She nudges my hip, swaying her body in time to the beat of the music. "It's Christmas," she roars in my ear. "You can't leave." She grins, winking at her boyfriend Leo as he eyes her like he's seconds away from jumping her bones.

"I want to stay, but I can't. Mrs. Griffin has a family she needs to get home to," I explain. It was sweet of her to keep Dad company while I attended this party at one of our old high school buddy's apartments in the downtown area, but I promised her I wouldn't be long.

Understanding washes over Xena's pretty face. "I keep forgetting. I'm sorry."

I shrug, draining the last dregs of my gin cocktail. "Some days, I forget too."

It's only been two months since Dad had a stroke, which left him paralyzed from the waist down, and only one month since I dropped out of UMaine to move back home to help care for him.

It's gradually sinking in—that the life I was leading, and the future I had planned, has all changed in the blink of an eye.

One brutal twist of fate altered my destiny, but I'm not crying over it.

It is what it is.

And I wouldn't have it any other way, because Dad has always been there for me. From day one, he has had my back, and there isn't anything I won't do for him.

There's no way I want strangers caring for him twenty-four-seven. As soon as we discovered his paralysis was permanent, I shed my old life and moved back home to Rydeville.

There was no dilemma. No anguished decision.

Dad needs me. He's my only flesh and blood.

And I'm home to look after him.

"At least, we get to hang out on the regular again," Xena says, pulling me into a hug. "I've missed you, girl."

Xena was my best friend all through school, and we were as close as sisters. But after we graduated from the public high school in Rydeville, our lives went in very different directions. Xena had decided back in freshman year that college wasn't in the cards for her. She walked straight into a job in her uncle's tattoo parlor and hasn't looked back since. My journey took me to the University of Maine and Isaac Sullivan, both now firmly relegated to the past.

"I'm glad we're reconnecting," I tell her, kissing her cheek. "And I'm so grateful for your support." Xena and I slotted back into an easy friendship, and I'd be lost without her daily messages and calls. She helps keep me sane on days when despair threatens to kick in.

"Anytime. You know I'm always here for you."

"Enjoy the rest of your night. Don't do anything I wouldn't do," I tease, waggling my brows as I watch the two guys circling her in anticipation. Only Xena would find two ripped, tatted, pierced hotties utterly devoted to her and take it all in her stride, like it's commonplace to have two boyfriends.

Lucky bitch. My neglected libido wails in my ear, missing regular sex, but that's the least of my worries right now.

I snatch my coat and my purse, wiggling my fingers at Bo and Leo and blowing one last kiss in my bestie's direction as I push my way through the crowd swarming the living room, out into the icy-cold night air.

The slicing sting skating along my cheeks is welcome after the overcrowded, overheated room, and I take my time putting my coat on, leaving it unbuttoned as I check my purse to ensure I have everything. My cell rings, and I pull it out, frowning as I spot the familiar number.

"Demi speaking."

"Oh, thank God," the male voice on the other end says.

"Danny? Is that you?" I ask, as I start walking, needing to confirm it's one of the security guards from the banking firm I work at because him calling me like this is beyond strange.

Usually, the building that houses Barron Banking and Financial Investment Services Limited is open twenty-four-seven with round-the-clock security personnel manning the fort, but I'd assumed things would change for the holidays. Guess I was wrong.

"It's me. I'm sorry to call you so late on Christmas, but I can't get hold of anyone else."

I button my coat with fingers that are rapidly turning

frozen, quickening my pace, while I keep the phone jammed between my ear and my shoulder. "What's going on?"

"I'm not sure." He sounds hesitant. "I've left messages for Mr. Barron, the president, and for Margaret Ann, but none of them are picking up, and I didn't know who else to call."

It must be bad if he's calling me. I've only been an employee for two weeks.

Although I followed in Dad's footsteps in my choice of accounting major, I never expected to end up where he had spent the last twenty-two years of his life working, and I certainly never expected to work for the man who tossed him so callously on his ass the minute he got sick.

But, as the saying goes, beggars can't be choosers. With mounting medical bills, we need the money. Pride doesn't come in to it. It's as simple as that.

"How can I help?"

"It's Mr. Barron's son. He arrived here a little while ago, and something is wrong. He was clutching a bottle of bourbon as he made his way up to the CEO's office. Someone needs to get here and ensure he's okay."

I don't recall babysitting rich pricks being part of my job description. "Can't you just put him in an Uber and send him home?"

"He won't talk to me. You're closer in age. Maybe, you might have more luck."

I snort. I've heard the rumors doing the rounds in the office about the boss's son. That he never dates. Just acquires fuck buddies. And, apparently, he has a thing for older women. I might be a few years older than Charlie Barron, but I very much doubt I'm his type or that I'd stand any chance at getting through to him.

Mr. Barron Senior is a coldhearted prick, and I've got zero desire to help him or his manwhore offspring. Not unless it's something I'm contractually obligated to fulfill. "Sorry, Danny. I need to get home to Dad, and I've had a couple gin cocktails, so even if I was available to help, I can't drive."

"I'll get Shirley, my wife, to pop round to your place, and I kinda already have a car on the way to pick you up," he sheepishly admits.

"I don't even know the guy, Danny!" I throw my hands in the air in exasperation even though he can't see me. "And what makes you think he'll talk to me?"

"Everyone loves you, Demi. And you'd be doing him a favor. He's drunk off his ass, and if his father discovers he showed up here in such a state, there'll be hell to pay. It can't hurt to try. Please."

I sigh, already knowing I'm going to regret this. But Danny is one of the few colleagues who was good to Dad after his stroke, one of the few who keeps in contact with him and makes the effort to visit, on the odd occasion. "Fine," I huff. "But I'm only doing this for you."

***

The driver pulls the Merc up in front of my new workplace, and I sigh. Lights are visible on the top-floor executive suite, and I can see Danny, his feet propped up on the security desk in the lobby, as I exit the back seat and walk toward the building.

I push through the doors, rubbing my frozen hands together as I smile at the gray-haired man who rises to meet me. "Merry Christmas, Demi. Thanks so much for this," Danny says, enveloping me in a fierce hug.

I stretch up and kiss his cheek. "Merry Christmas, Danny. It sucks you have to work."

He shrugs. "It's not so bad. My shift only started a couple

hours ago, so I got to spend the day with my family. I don't mind working the graveyard shift, someone's got to do it, and the extra money will come in handy."

"You're one of the good guys, Danny. Now, I see why my dad respects you so much."

His cheeks stain, and it's adorable. "Tell the old man Merry Christmas from me."

"I will." I smile. "And you owe me!" I tease as I stride toward the elevator bank with purpose.

I lean against the back of the elevator, watching the numbers rise as we shoot to the top of the building, wondering what the hell I've gotten myself into. This is crazy, and it could end up backfiring on me in a major way. Still, I'm here now, so I might as well see it through. I run my fingers through my long, dark tresses, unknotting the tangles the wind put there, as the doors open and I step out onto the executive level.

Everyone who works up here is in the executive secretarial pool, providing personal assistance to the various presidents and VPs. Unluckily for me, the CEO—Charles Barron the Second—needed a new assistant because the woman who worked with him for the past twenty years just retired, and I got the gig.

It's not the best use of my talents, but accounting jobs are in scarce supply, especially for college dropouts. It was either nepotism or guilt that swung the scales in my favor, I'm guessing, but my stellar college record no doubt helped too. I plan to work hard to show I deserve this job on my own merits, that I'm capable of more than this position, and I belong here in my own right, not just because my dad used to be their financial controller.

It kills me looking at that man's face every day knowing how he treated my father, but I've perfected the art of disguise, hiding my true thoughts and feelings, so Charles Barron doesn't see how much I despise him.

When Dad first had his stroke, there was talk of brain damage. The company was quick to jump on that, using it as an excuse to terminate Dad's employment. Sure, he got a decent severance package, but that's already dwindling with the mounting medical bills. Thankfully, there was no brain damage, but the ink was already dry on the paperwork, the payoff sitting in Dad's bank account, and there was little that could be done then to alter the outcome. After how callously Dad was treated, I didn't want him returning anyway.

I can stick it out until I gain some experience under my belt and find something better.

The main lights are switched on, and I walk past empty workstations with a growing sense of trepidation. When I reach my workstation, I notice the door to Mr. Barron's office is ajar. I remove my coat and place it and my purse on my desk as a shrill cry rings out in the solemn quiet. I gulp over the sudden lump in my throat as I lift my head, glancing at the door in front of me where the cry emanated from. Another anguished cry pricks my eardrums, the thread of pain evident in the strangled sobs, and it guts me.

When I got the call about Dad, I'll never forget the panic, sheer terror, and caustic pain that ripped my insides apart. I was so scared he would die alone in that hospital bed, and when I arrived to find him stable, I cried my eyes out in a mix of relief and fear, because I knew, in that moment, that everything had changed.

This man's sobs reach a hand inside me, squeezing my heart and crushing my lungs until it feels like I'm the one in pain.

I inch toward the door softly, pressing my ear up close. More sobs ring out, and even though I probably should pretend

I haven't heard, I can't ignore the fact I have. I don't know Charlie Barron, and he'll probably die of embarrassment if he discovers I've heard him crying, but I can't turn my back on anyone in need, no matter how undeserving they might seem, so I push the door open and step into the room without any further hesitation.

The room is bathed in a dim glow from the desktop lamp, the only illumination lighting up the space. The shadowy figure on the couch, at the other side of the room, stills at my sudden presence. His broad shoulders heave as he fights to compose himself. After a few beats, he lifts his head, staring in my direction.

With tentative steps, I walk toward him. The closer I get, the sharper his features become. I only caught a fleeting glimpse of him one time when he visited his father, and even though Charlie Barron is young, he's definitely all man and one of the hottest guys I've seen in a long time.

Sorry, Isaac.

I force those thoughts aside as I approach him. His red-rimmed eyes and tearstained cheeks confirm the sobs were coming from him. His suit jacket is thrown over the arm of the couch, his white shirt unbuttoned at the top and his tie hanging loose around his neck. His hair is in disarray, as if he was repeatedly dragging his fingers through the dark strands.

I come to a halt in front of him, my heart beating so loud I'm sure he must hear it. He tips his chin up, staring at me with a frown, and I'm cursing my bleeding heart. *Why didn't I just tell Danny a firm no? Or why didn't I bail the instant I heard Charlie's cries?* But I didn't do either. I'm here now, and I need to say something. I clear my throat. "Are you... Is everything okay?"

He stares at me, and even though the lighting is low, I can detect the growing curiosity in his piercing green eyes as he drinks in my features. His gaze roams my face, and the longer my question remains unanswered, the more tense the situation seems.

"Who are you?" he asks, in a hoarse voice, after what feels like eternity.

"I'm Demi Alexander. Your father's new personal assistant," I confirm.

Pain slashes across his face, and a muscle clenches in his jaw as he visibly struggles to hold it together.

What the hell is going on?

Taking a chance, I sit down beside him, angling my body so we're facing one another. "What's happened? And where is your father? What are you doing in his office after ten on Christmas night?" *And why are you crying?* That's what I really want to ask, but I can't ever forget my place. Charlie Barron, a.k.a. Charles Barron the Third is the heir apparent, and he will one day be my boss.

My breath stutters in my throat when he lifts his hand, brushing his fingers across my cheek, leaving a wake of fiery tremors zipping along my skin. He stares into my eyes, and I see a world of pain reflected in his gaze. "Dead," he whispers, his warm, earthy breath feathering across my face. "My father is dead."

My eyes pop wide, and my heart beats frantically behind my rib cage. "What?" I splutter, staring at him to see if this is some twisted joke. I mean, I loathe the man and everything he stands for, but that doesn't mean I wanted him dead. I know what it's like to lose a parent, and even though I never knew my mom, I still feel the pain of her loss acutely. And even thinking of losing Dad splinters my heart into pieces. I spent hours thinking he might be gone, and the pain was unimaginable, so I have an inkling of what this man is feeling. It's no wonder he was in tears. "How did it happen?"

He shakes his head, biting down hard on his lip. "He's gone. The specifics don't matter." His fingers drop lower, skimming my jawline, and his eyes latch onto my mouth. He trails his fingers along my jaw and then down onto my neck, and each sweeping touch awakens something dormant inside me.

Heat courses through me from his touch and the intense way he's looking at me, and raw need surges to the surface. It's been years since I've felt such potent yearning, and the guy is barely touching me. "I'm sorry," I say, meaning it even if I hated his father. I can see how upset he is over it.

"You look..." He trails off, exhaling heavily, shaking his head, and dropping his hands from my face as he reaches for the half-empty bottle of bourbon on the coffee table.

His lips suction around the neck of the bottle, and he drinks heartily before passing it to me. I'm not much of a drinker, but it'd seem rude to decline, and it's already a freaking strange night. So, I take the bottle, and we pass it back and forth without speaking. He leans back in the couch, spreading his legs and lounging more comfortably, as I kick off my boots and tuck my knees into my chest, grateful I chose to wear leggings under my dress.

He watches my every move like a skillful hunter eyeing his prey. With every mouthful of bourbon I swallow, my limbs grow more relaxed, and I find myself silently encouraging him to move in for the kill.

Like I said, it's a strange night.

"Why did you come here?" I ask after a while, sucking in a gasp as our fingers brush when I pass the bottle back to him.

"I had nowhere else to go," he admits before bringing the bottle to his mouth. I watch his plump lips wrap around the bottle, and the way his throat works as he drinks is hella sexy.

I totally understand how this guy has earned his rep. I don't sleep around, and I can count on one hand the number of guys

I've been with, yet I'd spread my legs for him in a heartbeat. Charlie exudes this sexy energy that draws me in, and I just know a night with him would be a night I'd never forget.

But I'm sensing there's a lot more to him than that. I barely know the guy; we haven't spoken more than a few sentences to one another, and yet I feel his vulnerability and his loneliness as potently as a slap to the face.

This guy is in a world of pain.

And maybe, it's my bleeding heart or the alcohol sloshing through my veins, or maybe, it's just *this guy*, but I want to eviscerate his pain. Even if it's only temporary.

I scoot closer to him, reaching out to cup his cheek. His skin is smooth and warm to the touch. "How can I help?"

His fingers wrap around my wrist, holding my hand to his face. He stares at me for an inordinate amount of time, and my chest heaves with anticipation. A crackle of electricity connects the space between us, and the more he stares at me, the more I want to throw caution to the wind.

"You can let me pretend," he croaks, as his eyes plead with me.

I quirk a brow, but he doesn't elaborate, skimming his gaze all over my body in a way that confirms his mind has gone to the same place mine has.

This is a bad idea.

A really, really bad idea.

Because if his dad is dead, that makes him my new boss, and he's grieving. He's not in his right mind. And I'm not in mine because this isn't who I am. Yet, in his presence, it's who I want to become.

"Okay." I'm pleased my voice comes out confident despite the way I'm trembling inside.

"You don't know what I'm asking," he adds, angling his head so he can suck my pinkie into his mouth.

I gasp as pleasurable warmth filters through my body, igniting every cell and nerve ending. "Show me," I beg, no longer able to keep the craving from my tone or my face.

Forcing my hand aside, he grips my face in his large palms and slams his mouth down on mine. Stars explode in vibrant bursts of color behind my eyelids as his lips devour me like he's been waiting years to taste me.

His lips glide with skill and precision against mine while he hauls me into his lap. His fingers dig into my hips as he pulls me against his erection, ensuring I feel how much he needs this. I run my fingers through his hair, pressing my chest against his, letting him know I'm right there with him.

His kisses grow more aggressive, and he punishes my mouth with a slew of drugging, bruising kisses. It's in direct contrast to the loving, gentle way Isaac used to kiss me, and as I cling to Charlie, biting and nipping at his lips, I know I've been in denial for far longer than I realized.

I'm on fire. Every part of me hums with expectation and need, so when he lifts my dress off me and unclips my bra, I offer no resistance. I moan into his hair as his hot mouth worships my bare breasts, his teeth grazing my nipples as he grinds his hips into mine. I rock against him, needing the friction against my achy core to sate my growing need.

In between hot kisses, we rip at our clothes until we're both naked, and he wastes no time rolling a condom on and yanking me roughly down on top of him. He's sitting up with his back against the arm of the couch as I straddle him.

I moan as his long, thick, hard length fills me up, and I'm immediately consumed in him. I bounce up and down on him, writhing and whimpering, as he moves his hips in sync with my movements. I place my hands on his shoulders as I fuck him, closing my eyes and tossing my hair back as he worships my breasts with his slick mouth while his cock slams inside me over and over again.

His fingers dig into my hips and he thrusts into me in savage strokes, gritting his teeth as he flexes his hips, driving harder and harder, as if he can't get deep enough. My climax is already building, surprising me, because I rarely orgasmed from sex with Isaac.

My head falls forward onto Charlie's shoulder as his arms wrap tightly around me and his wicked lips leave my breasts, trailing a line of firm kisses along my collarbone and up my neck. He nips at my skin with his teeth, and jolts of pleasurable pain ripple over my heightened flesh. My skin is a live wire, and his fingers are like volts of electricity as they glide across my body, singeing in every place they touch.

Without warning, he lowers me to my back and lifts my left leg up over his shoulder. His cock sinks even deeper at this angle, and I cry out as the pressure in my core builds to a crescendo. He fucks me raw, pounding into me like he's exorcising his demons, and perhaps, he is. He exudes aggression and frustration with every pivot of his hips, every bruising thrust, as he ruins me for all other men.

Charlie may be young, but he's clearly very experienced in all things sexual, and I'm riding the crest of that experience as he continues fucking me like a madman, inciting a flurry of new sensations inside me.

He buries his face in my neck, sucking on my skin in a way I know will leave a mark, but I couldn't care less at this moment. I grab hold of his firm ass cheeks, pulling him in closer, needing more. My hands roam the muscled planes of his back and his broad shoulders, and I scrape my nails along his sweat-slickened skin, delighting in the fact I'm leaving my mark on him too.

There is something so primal, so intimate, about the way

we're fucking that is entirely new to me, and it could easily become an addiction.

I drag my lips in a line across his chest, nipping at his skin, and he growls out his encouragement. I inhale his scent like it's the oxygen I need to breathe while I continue my assault on his impressive chest, caving to my inner beast as I'm rough with him too. I can't get enough of him, and I need to come, yet I long to prolong this moment too. I can't marry those conflicting thoughts, but I don't have to, because my body takes control, barreling toward the most orgasmic explosion of my life. I scream his name as I come, my inner walls gripping his cock tight as I shatter, drowning in exquisite waves of intense pleasure, coming apart and being remade at the same time.

Charlie lifts my other leg over his shoulder and picks up his pace, thrusting inside me like he'll die if he doesn't come. His face is still cradled in my neck as he slams inside me at this punishing angle, and I know the moment he reaches his peak because his entire body locks up tight and he emits an animalistic roar birthed from someplace deep. Then he's jerking and pulsing inside me, his body trembling and shaking over me as he comes.

"I love you, Abby," he whispers in my ear, and I stop breathing. Blood rushes to my head, and a heavy weight presses down on my chest at his words.

You can let me pretend.

His earlier words reverberate in my mind as I curse my stupidity. I thought he meant he wanted to pretend everything was okay, that his father hadn't died, but I got it completely wrong, and now I feel sick. Nausea twists and turns in my gut as I crash back to Earth with a bang.

He hasn't been with me in this.

The intimacy and pleasure I felt between us as we made

love was a lie. No wonder he's barely kissed me. Barely looked at me.

He hasn't been present.

He's been with *her*.

This Abby woman.

Whoever she may be.

He's stopped moving, and the only sounds in the room are our joint heavy breaths. I was under no illusion. I knew this was only a one-time thing. We're from two different worlds, and we both needed this for various reasons. But it still meant something to me. And now, I'm hurt. I feel cheap. Used. As irreplaceable as a worthless whore.

I shouldn't be surprised. His father is a cruel prick with little regard for other people's feelings too. It stands to reason his son would be the same. I shove at his shoulders as tears prick my eyes. I'm such a gullible fool. "Get off me."

He lifts his head from my shoulder, staring at my face with a puckered brow.

I glare at him as I push his shoulders again. I need to put as much distance between us as I can, and I can't get away from him fast enough.

He climbs off me like an elegant gazelle, standing over me with a frown, watching as I grab my clothes and hastily pull them on.

"Did I hurt you?" he asks as I yank my leggings up my legs.

I snort, purposely not looking at him. He's standing there in all his naked glory, and I know one look will have my ovaries purring like a kitten in heat. I've always prided myself on my ability to look beyond the exterior and find real attraction buried underneath, but tonight, I threw all my beliefs in the toilet for a tryst with a hot guy who was in pain. Only, the joke's on me, because I could have been any warm body. I bet he doesn't even remember *my* name.

I slip my feet into my boots and look up at his handsome face, finding him ugly now. "Who is Abby?"

He visibly pales, and his Adam's apple jumps in his throat. A few seconds tick by, and it's obvious he's not going to answer.

Asshole.

I prod my finger into his chest. "You fucked me imagining I was her. I at least deserve to know who she is."

Air whooshes out of his mouth as he claws his hands through his hair. Torment is etched across his face, but I'm not falling for it this time. I have no idea what's going on here, but I want no part of it.

"She's my wife," he finally says, and all the blood drains from my face.

"I..." I falter, unable to form words to convey my horror at what's just happened. Bile travels up my throat. I abhor cheating. It's a major no-no in my book. And this asshole—my new boss—has just made me an accomplice to adultery. I struggle to breathe over the pain settling on my chest. "You make me sick," I say, fighting angry tears. "I would never have had sex with you if I'd known you were married." Like, the guy's only eighteen or nineteen, and none of my colleagues told me he was married. In fact, if the rumors are to be believed, he's the quintessential playboy bachelor. I don't understand.

"We only got married today," he says, adding to my horror.

I slap a hand over my mouth, staring at him in shock. A few tears sneak out of my eyes, dripping down my face, but I angrily swipe at them as rage overtakes every other emotion I've been feeling.

I've just been fucked in more ways than one. This is a clusterfuck of life-altering possibilities, but I can't lose this job. Dad is relying on me, and I'm not letting him down.

"This never happened!" I blurt when I remove my hand from my mouth. "And if you attempt to terminate my employment, I will slap you with a sexual harassment lawsuit quicker than you can frog-march me out the door."

"I would never do that," he says, quick to reassure me.

But I'm sure the apple doesn't fall too far from the tree, and I'm not buying it.

He pulls on his pants as I storm toward the door. I clutch the door handle, talking to him over my shoulder. "See that you don't, or I'll make your life hell," I promise, hoping he can't see through my bravado.

"It's in my interests to keep this secret," he adds, and my disgust elevates another notch.

I nod tersely as I turn my head to face him. "From now on, it's strictly professional, and we breathe a word to no one." A fleeting thought crosses my mind.

I could blackmail him for my silence.

God knows we need the money.

But I dismiss the idea as quickly as it came to me. That's not who I am. And no good comes from taking dirty money.

"Agreed." He stares through me as if I don't exist. And, I guess, to him, I don't.

"Go home to your wife, Charlie," I hiss as I whip the door open and stalk outside, wishing I could rewind time and erase the last couple hours from my life.

Chapter One
Charlie – Nine Months Later

I keep my head down, jotting notes as the professor's grating tone projects around the packed auditorium. With all these people here, you'd think it'd be easy to avoid my former friends, but every time I look sideways, I spot Abby or Drew or that asshole Anderson. Doesn't help that Drew, Shandra, and Anderson's buddy Lauder are all business majors, like me, and we share a bunch of the same classes. Thank fuck I'm only here part-time. If I was forced to confront them all the time, I'd probably drop out.

My cell pings just as the professor uploads our new assignment on the board and draws the lecture to a close. I glance at the text with a scowl, knowing I'll be heading into a shitstorm when I step into the office in an hour.

As much as I dread arriving at Rydeville University every morning for classes, I feel physically ill arriving at the high-rise glass building in downtown Boston every lunchtime, because I know *her* face is one of the first I'll see.

One look at Demi and I'm reminded of my biggest failures.

Of the night that set everything in motion.

And I fucking hate her for the part she played in my eventual downfall.

Everything about her ties my stomach into painful knots, and if I could get away with firing her sexy ass, I'd have done it a long time ago. But she's got fire in her belly, and I don't want to call her bluff. Instead, I go out of my way to make her life a living hell hoping someday soon she'll get the hint and resign.

I tap out a quick reply to the CEO before tucking my phone into the inside pocket of my suit jacket.

When freshman year commenced a few weeks ago, I used to wear jeans every day and drop by the house to change before heading into the office. But I couldn't give a flying fuck what anyone thinks of me anymore. So, I attend lectures in my dress suit, sticking out like a sore thumb, but I have zero fucks to give. I'm not here to make friends. I'm here to get a business degree so I can use the learning to mold myself into the CEO my dad always wanted me to become.

I owe him that much.

Actually, I owe him so much more, but the rest is a work in progress.

Dad's second in command, the guy who was president before I was thrust into the role, has stepped into Dad's CEO shoes for the time being. Dad left stipulations in his will in case something like this happened. Even in death, he's ensuring I continue my education and my training, and I'll only assume the CEO role once I've graduated with my degree and gotten a firm handle on every aspect of business operations.

It's unnecessary. I could take control now and learn on the job. This degree is a checkbox exercise. One, I must, unfortunately, achieve, in order to gain control of the family business.

It pisses me off. Everyone knows I'm the boss. In everything but name. But I'll play this charade because the lawyers tell me it's the only way I'll get my hands on the company, and it's been in our family for too many generations to let it fall into the board members' hands under my watch.

I sling my laptop bag over my shoulder and take the stairs two at a time, following the other students out of the auditorium. The hallway is teeming with people as I walk with purpose toward the food court to grab some lunch to take with me to the office.

The food court is buzzing, as usual, but I grab a sandwich, a bottle of water, a bag of chips, and some fruit and line up to pay for it.

"Drew, please. Come on. Stop shutting me out."

My ears prick up as I hear Shandra Farrell's sultry, pleading tone. I cast a quick glance over my shoulder, spotting her with Drew Manning, my former best friend, in the line a couple of places behind. I turn around before they notice me.

"Shandra. I can't do this. I've said all I needed to. Please just drop it."

"I won't wait for you forever," she says, and I detect the sadness and longing in her voice.

I wonder if I sounded that pitiful when I was pining after Abby.

I shake my head as the memories lay seize to my brain, disgusted at myself all over again.

"I don't want you to wait for me. I can't give you what you need—now or anytime in the future," Drew says. "Just let it go."

"Fine." Her tone is snippy. "It's your loss, Drew. It's certainly not mine." Her heels make a clacking sound on the tile floor as she storms off.

I reach the register and hand over my tray, glancing in Drew's direction as the girl rings it up.

He's rubbing his temples, his brow creased, clearly troubled. His eyes lift, and our gazes lock for a few seconds. He jerks his head in acknowledgement, and I give him a cursory nod in reply before turning around and handing my student meal card to the girl behind the register.

I don't look at him as I walk away, and he makes no effort to talk to me. I've long since passed the point of caring. I don't need him or anyone in my life.

I'm an island, and that's just how I like it.

That way, there's no one to disappoint if I fuck up again.

Not that I intend to.

What happened was a momentary lapse in judgment, and I will ensure it never happens again. No woman will ever penetrate the steel walls I've rebuilt around my heart, and that's a promise I've made to myself. One I fully intend to keep.

I've just reached the doors when she calls out to me. "Charlie! Wait!"

"Fuck," I mumble under my breath, closing my eyes for a second, as I silently beg her to let it go. But Abby is stubborn as shit when she gets something in her mind, and I know my silent prayer is in vain.

A guy plows into my side as I turn around. "Sorry, man."

I ignore him, moving off to the side so I'm not blocking the entrance, watching as the brunette beauty who used to play a starring role in my dreams comes charging toward me.

She's wearing skinny black jeans and a black-and-white off-the-shoulder sweater, and even though she's wearing high-heeled boots, I still tower over her when she catches up to me.

"You're sitting with us." Her glare dares me to challenge her decision as she grabs on to my arm, attempting to pull me forward.

"No. I'm not." I shuck out of her hold, sending her a challenging glare of my own. "No one wants me at that table, especially me."

She crosses her arms and juts out her hip in defiance. "*I* want you there."

"Why? It will only cause an argument between you and him."

I still find it hard calling him her husband. The word always seems to stick in my throat even though I've accepted the situation and the fact they are crazy in love.

Abby is obviously happy. It radiates from her every pore. And I'm happy for her. Genuinely, I am. All I ever wanted was for her to be free of the hold that bastard Michael Hearst had over her and to be happy and in love.

But I wanted her to be happy and in love with *me*.

However, we don't always get what we want.

"Because you're our friend and it's time we left the past in the past. We've all made mistakes. You're not alone in that."

I watch him approaching from over her shoulder, and I'm not surprised at the look of displeasure on his face. There is no love lost between Kaiden Anderson and me, and everyone knows it. Even Abby. But she seems hellbent on ignoring that critical fact.

"My mistakes got my father killed, not to mention the danger I placed you in," I tell her as I watch him advance. "You should want nothing to do with me." I'm not looking for sympathy. I'm merely stating the facts.

"Abby." Kaiden places his hand on his wife's shoulder. "Leave it."

Her eyes narrow as she turns to her husband. "You know better than to tell me what to do."

"You can't force Charlie to sit with us if he doesn't want to." He looks me straight in the eye. "You can join us anytime. Don't hold back on my account." Abby leans into his side, smiling at him in a way that sours my stomach. He returns her smile, rubbing his thumb along her lower lip, and some unspoken communication passes between them. It's an intimate moment between two people who exist only for each other, and I'm done.

"I just want to be left alone," I tell her, gripping the strap of my bag tighter.

She grabs my elbow before I've turned my back on them. "You took a bullet for me, Charlie, and I will never forget that. You asked for time, and I've given you time. But if either of you think I'm dropping this, you don't know me at all."

My lips twitch of their own volition, and Kaiden slants a dark glare in my direction. He's such an ass.

He won.

He stole her heart right out from under me, and he has her —hook, line, and sinker—so he could at least drop the evil eye.

But I doubt he will ever see me as anything more than an enemy. And I've got no one to blame but myself. Because I fucked up. I fucked up bad, and there's no coming back from it.

I walk away without uttering another word, knowing Abby won't give up, but I have bigger problems to deal with today.

Figuring out what to do about my ex-obsession is a problem for a different day.

"Simon Reed called again," Demi says, hovering in front of my desk like the annoying pest she's become. "That's the tenth time in two days."

"I can count," I drawl, placing my laptop bag on top of my desk alongside the paper bag containing my lunch. "What time is the executive meeting set for?" I ask, sinking into my chair and powering up my laptop.

"Three fifteen in the main conference room."

"Fine. Get me a coffee and get out."

Her lips thin. "Would it kill you to treat me with some respect?"

"Greedy sluts don't command respect or warrant attention. You are as insignificant as the dirt underneath my shoe. I know your level of intelligence is questionable, but surely, you're smart enough to understand that."

"You know I have ample grounds to report you for the way you speak to me."

I fully expect she's been keeping a log of every insult, every threat, and every attempt I make to force her into quitting. But the more I antagonize her, the more she digs her heels in. She's got grit, and I add it to the list of things I hate about her, because she isn't making this easy for me—at all.

I snort out a laugh, not looking up at her. It drives her insane when I refuse to make eye contact. It's just an added reason to avoid looking at her perfect face. "Knock yourself out, sweetheart. It's no skin off my back if you want to embarrass yourself. Perhaps, I'll make a complaint of my own."

I enter my password and log in to the system. "Taking advantage of the president when he was drunk, and grieving, is surely a sackable offense." I lift the handset on my desktop phone. "Let me call the chief human relations officer, and she can decide."

It's a dick move, and we both know it.

She grabs the phone from my hand, slamming it down hard, and the air ignites with her simmering rage.

She would love to tell me to go fuck myself. But she can't.

Sucks to be Demi Alexander.

I smirk, breaking my self-imposed rules and eyeballing her.

Fuck. *Why does she have to be so drop-dead gorgeous with those big brown eyes, pouty lips, and lustrous dark hair?* I still remember how she felt as I thrust up inside her. How hot it was when her pussy gripped my cock as she fell apart underneath me. How sexy she looked with her flushed skin and how hard I was with every little breathy moan that fell from her plump lips.

My cock stirs to life behind my pants, but that's nothing new. Working in such proximity to her is daily torture, but it's a punishment I accept. I deserve to languish in hell for all the heinous things I've done.

I've ripped my family apart.

Destroyed every friendship I had.

Pushed away the only girl I've ever loved.

And the woman fuming in front of me is a daily reminder of how I fucked things up with Abby. Demi became the barrier Abby hid behind. It didn't matter that she didn't know her name. She knew she existed. That I'd sought solace in her arms, her body, the night my father died, the same night we were married. And Abby used every opportunity to rub my nose in it.

If only Demi hadn't shown up here Christmas night.

If only I hadn't slept with her.

Maybe, just maybe, I might have actually stood a chance with Abby.

Chapter Two
Demi

"Asshole. Douche canoe. Giant bag of dicks. Jerk-off. Dickwad." I'm murmuring to myself as I leave the office later that evening, thinking of different ways to describe that fucktard of a boss of mine. I blow a kiss at Danny, through the glass, before walking in the direction of the bar Bo works at, tapping out a quick message to Xena to let her know I'm on my way.

This is Mrs. Griffin's late shift and the only night I have a few hours to myself after work. Dad organized it with her. I know he worries about me. That he feels guilty. And he uses every opportunity to get me out of the house.

I only love him more for it.

Especially after last week's newest bombshell.

Tears sting my eyes, and a messy ball of emotion clogs my throat as I think of the latest medical diagnosis.

It's so unfair.

Dad grew up in a house devoid of love, and when he finally found it, with a woman he adored and cherished, she was stolen from him the day I was born. He sacrificed his career and his personal needs to ensure he was always there for me, and now, at a time when he should finally be reclaiming control of his life, he's on borrowed time, thanks to the fucking cancer they've just discovered ravaging his failing body.

He won't be around to grow old. To walk me up the aisle. Or play with his grandchildren.

I swipe at the hot tears streaming down my face as I cross the road toward the bar. I need to get my shit together. Crying over it isn't going to help. I need a plan of action, and I need one fast if I'm to save Dad before it's too late.

The bar is busy for a Thursday evening, and I fight my way through the mob to the far end of the room where Xena is perched on a stool, eye-fucking boyfriend numero uno. I call him that because Bo was on the scene first. From what Xena told me, they dated for four months before she met Leo and fell head over heels in love with him too.

Some girls have all the luck.

"Hey, babe. Sorry I'm late. The a-hole made me stay behind to finish a file for him." I slide onto the empty stool beside my bestie.

"Our offer still stands," Bo supplies, sliding a beer in my direction.

I accept it gratefully, smiling. "I appreciate that, but I don't want you and Leo getting in trouble for putting the beatdown on the jerk. He's not worth doing time for."

"We'd only do time if we were caught." Bo winks as he stacks glasses.

"Trust me, this guy has more money than he knows what to do with. He'd sic some PI on the case, and he'd find you guys in a heartbeat." I wouldn't want that on my conscience.

Besides, violence isn't the answer.

Even if I'm tempted, daily, to punch Charlie in his smug face.

"And Barron's mixed up with that Parkhurst place," Xena adds before bringing the bottle of beer to her lips. "I don't want either of my guys getting involved in that shit." She tosses her long purple locks over her shoulder as she pins Bo with a cautionary look.

"How'd you know about that?" I ask.

"I'm not just a pretty face," she jokes, shoulder checking me. "It was splashed all over the news back when the FBI raided the place. I saw an article online with a list of members, and the Barrons were on it."

I'm well aware, because I had reason to conduct my own online snooping. Plus, there was a ton of gossip in the office at the time all that shit went down. But the board of directors shut it down straightaway, issuing a press conference stating the integrity of the company and its founding owners was above reproach.

Parkhurst was apparently a front for some elite organization made up of wealthy pricks who thought the rules didn't apply to them. It's not much of a surprise to discover the Barrons were a part of it.

Her arm goes around me automatically. "Let's get fucked up and forget about your jackass boss even if he is hot as fuck with a monster cock."

I spit my beer all over the counter. "Xena!" I hiss, glancing around.

Her arm drops away from me.

"This place isn't far from the office. Anyone could be listening." I'm regretting telling her everything that happened that night, because it's clear she can't hold shit.

"When you say monster cock, how big are we talking?" Bo asks, grinning salaciously as he leans his elbows on the counter, staring at me.

"Remind me again why I confided in you?" I give Xena the stink eye. It's only half fake.

"Because I'm your bestest friend and you love me." She tweaks my nose, and I elbow her in the ribs.

"You're lucky I love you, because you're a lousy secret keeper."

She shrugs. "Keeping secrets only leads to trouble. It's best to get everything out on the table."

"There's a difference between sharing secrets that need to be told and keeping a confidence, Xena." I arch a brow, sending her a pointed look.

I told her what happened that night in good faith, and I was pissed when I found out she'd told her boyfriends. I know there was no malice in it. She explained she doesn't like keeping shit from the guys, and a part of me respects and admires her for it. And it's not like she blabbed to strangers, but I still didn't appreciate it.

I'm not the type to kiss and tell, but I was furious and upset Christmas night after being an innocent participant in adultery, and I needed to vent.

"You're right," she agrees without protest, "and I should've explained that I don't keep secrets from the guys before you confided in me."

"Well, this is one secret that needs to be kept hidden, because I need this shitty job now more than ever." I take a long swig of my drink, watching Bo and Xena trade worried expressions.

"How bad is it?" Xena asks, in a softer tone, when I put my beer down.

"Stage four," I whisper, and I hate how my lower lip wobbles when I'm trying so hard to be strong.

"Shit." She grabs hold of my hand. "Is there anything we can do to help?"

"Short of winning the lottery, there isn't anything that can be done." I hate admitting it, but it's the truth. "I'd love to know who came up with the saying 'money doesn't buy you happiness' because I'd like to punch them in the face. What a crock of shit," I add, angrily picking at the label on my beer. "I guess it was coined by some rich bastard who has no idea what it's like to not have enough money, because I'll tell you, if we had money for that experimental drug, and it stopped the cancer from spreading, and it gave Dad a few more years to live, I'd be fucking ecstatic."

"How much is it?" Bo asks, wiping the counter down and purposely ignoring the guy at his back calling for his attention.

"More than we can afford."

"We can fundraise," he suggests. "I know the owner would let us use the bar." He shoots me a sympathetic look as he walks off to serve the now irate customer.

"And my uncle would let us organize something at the shop," Xena adds.

"Thank you, and I might take you up on that." I drink another mouthful of beer.

"We should brainstorm." She taps her fingers on the counter, looking off into space. "You could stay over at our place Saturday night after the club, and we can put our heads together over breakfast Sunday morning?"

I haven't been out on a Saturday night in months, and I'm only going because it's my twenty-second birthday, and Xena, the sneaky cow, went behind my back to Dad to arrange the night out when I politely declined his previous suggestion.

"I'll see if that's okay with Mrs. Griffin." I was planning on coming home even though Dad's caregiver is already staying the night. If she's okay staying a couple of hours extra on Sunday morning, I can swing it.

Truth is, I need all the help I can get, and four brains are definitely better than one.

"That asshole Barron should be coughing up for the treatment and all your dad's medical bills."

"It happened before he became president," I say although I'm not defending him, per se. "But you're right, the company has a lot to answer for."

Strictly speaking, they didn't do anything illegal with the information we had to hand at the time. After Dad had his stroke, the doctors believed he might have brain damage. The company grabbed that assumption and ran with it, approaching Dad with an exit offer considering he was now incapable of working.

They gave him a generous severance package and washed their hands of him with a clear conscience.

But they could've changed their minds after the test results came back clear of brain injury. Because my dad gave them years and years of his loyal service, and when he needed them to have his back, they kicked him to the curb without a second glance. If he still had his premium medical insurance, the cancer bombshell we've just been hit with would be different because he'd be able to enter the trial and he might have a fighting chance. Without it, there is little hope, and it's just one more reason to hate the offspring of the late CEO.

"Hey, Dad." I lean down and kiss his cheek. "How are you today?" I plop down on the couch beside him, taking his hands in mine.

"All the better for seeing my sweet girl," he replies, squeezing my fingers. I hate how frail his touch has become.

How lined his face now seems. How gaunt his cheekbones are. And how his clothes hang from his much thinner frame.

Dad had adapted after the stroke, and he was learning to live with it. But now, the cancer bomb has been dropped in his lap, and he's struggling to stay positive. I hate that I didn't see it. That we didn't have the money to go for monthly checkups instead of biannual appointments. Perhaps, they might have caught it earlier. When it could be treated more easily and without resorting to some new experimental drug trial which we've been told is his only chance at prolonging his life.

"How was your day?" he adds. "I hope young Charles is treating my princess good."

I smother a snort. I don't want Dad worrying, so I've told him nothing about the way Charlie Barron treats me. "He's a good boss," I lie.

"He was always a good kid," Dad says. "Troubled, but his heart seemed to be in the right place."

Oh, Dad. If only you knew.

"You two have a lot in common."

My mouth falls open. "Like what?" I splutter.

"He's had to grow up fast too. He's carrying the burden for his family the same way you are."

My features soften. "You're not a burden, Dad. I love you, and I'm right where I want to be."

Tears fill his eyes, and a lump the size of a bus wedges in my throat.

"When my time comes, I'll die a happy man knowing I did one right thing in this world. You make me so very proud, Demitria. Please don't let this change you."

"I hate the unfairness of it all," I truthfully admit. "You're the best person I know, Dad, and you don't deserve this. Deserve any of the hardships life has thrown at you."

"My life has been full, honey, and I'll die with no regrets

because I got to share my life with you and my Luana. I'm luckier than most."

A strangled sob pierces through the air, and we both look around. Mrs. Griffin is standing in the doorway, clutching her chest, her navy-blue eyes flooded with moisture. "I'm sorry," she cries. "I didn't mean to eavesdrop, but I just wanted to have a word with Demi before I left, and I didn't want to interrupt such a beautiful moment."

"It's fine, Nora," Dad says. "Don't ever feel the need to apologize around here."

"I'm good to talk now," I say, kissing Dad on the cheek again. "Do you need me to get you anything, Dad?"

"I'm good, sweetheart. I'll just watch the end of this documentary before bed."

I squeeze his hand before I walk out into the kitchen with his caregiver.

"Your father is one of a kind, Demi," she says. "Truly a beautiful, gentle soul. I'm not sure I could be quite as understanding in his condition."

"Nor me," I agree, switching the coffee pot on. "He inspires me every day." I might not share his belief or his faith in a god who would do this to him, but the way he's handled things since his stroke is genuinely admirable. I really do believe in positive mental attitude and my dad has that in spades.

"I filled that new script today," she says, pointing at the clear plastic box on top of the counter. "And I divided it into the different days and times." She opens the box, taking out a blue and a white tablet. "He's to take these with water just before bed."

I nod, taking them from her. "I'll make sure he takes them."

"And he now has to take those two green ones, in addition to his usual meds, after his breakfast."

I bob my head. "Got it." Mrs. Griffin arrives early on weekdays so I can leave for work, but I'm Dad's primary caregiver over the weekends, so I need to be fully up to speed on this stuff.

"Okay, kiddo." She presses a kiss to the top of my head. "I'm off. I'll see you bright and early tomorrow morning."

"Thank you, Nora." I hug her. "I mean it. Thank you for everything. We're so lucky to have found you."

When Dad was in the hospital, after his stroke, I had placed signs in a few local stores looking for a caregiver while I figured out what to do about school. Nora was the first woman to make contact, and I warmed to her immediately. Dad did too. And we both knew we didn't need to interview anyone else. Her credentials were amazing, she lived locally, and we both just got a good feeling about her.

"It works both ways, honey," she says, returning my hug. "I'm glad to have you and your dad in my life." She shucks out of my embrace, tenderly brushing hair out of my face. "I consider you family, and I hope you know I'll always be here for you."

Because once Dad is gone, I'm all that's left. Everyone else is dead.

She doesn't say it, but she doesn't have to.

Dad's words return to me, and I suppose that's something else Charlie and I have in common.

We're both alone, because his dad is dead and his mom and sister have moved to Arizona, and, if the rumors are to be believed, he's not on speaking terms with either of them.

But that is where the similarities end.

On this occasion, I think Dad is wrong, because Charlie and I are nothing alike—except for the mutual hatred we share for one another.

Chapter Three
Charlie

"We can always go back to my place if you're not enjoying it here," Emilia purrs in my ear while her hand inches higher up my thigh.

"We're staying," I grit out, removing her hand before she touches my dick. If she notices how grumpy I am tonight, she doesn't mention it. I suspect she's holding out hope I'm looking for more than casual fucking because I've called on her a lot more lately. It's only because I'm low on options and too lazy to actively recruit new fuck buddies. But there isn't a hope in hell she and I will ever be anything more.

In fact, after tonight, I think I'll be crossing her off my list permanently. I've grown tired of fucking her, and she's lost all appeal.

Strobe lights crisscross overhead as hypnotic beats bounce off the walls of the club. I've never been to this part of town before, and it's my first foray in here, but I like it. It's a far cry from the glitzy places I'm used to frequenting with the elite, but I like the industrial-type styling and the grungy vibe in the air.

The clientele is a strange bunch, and I'm sure this place has seen its fair share of fights and deals, but I'm cool with that. It's tame compared to the shit I've seen at elite events and stuff I've been forced to participate in at Parkhurst.

"You seem jumpy," Emilia adds, trailing her hands up my chest. Her long, blonde hair falls in straight lines across one shoulder as she repositions herself on the stool. "And you're so tense." She digs her fingers into the corded muscle of my shoulders, and I flinch, recoiling at her touch.

"Stop." My face is a mask of indifference as I push her hands away. "Sit down, drink your drink, and only talk when I tell you to." I'm being a total prick, but I don't care. Her inane chatter is giving me a headache. I should've come here alone, but I'm not sure what to expect, and I thought she might come in handy.

Coming to this club was an impulsive decision. One I'm regretting. But I'm here now, so I might as well wait for Demi to arrive.

When I overheard her making plans to celebrate her birthday, I had no intention of showing my face. But I was climbing the walls at home, bored out of my skull, rattling around that large, empty house, and I craved a change of scenery.

I pull out my cell, discreetly checking the app, pleased to see she's only a mile away.

Adding a tracking device to her private cell is a blatant invasion of her privacy and something that would land me in hot water with the board of directors if it ever got out. But this isn't my first surveillance rodeo. I know how to cover my tracks, and there's no way anyone could trace it back to me.

I told myself I installed it so I could fuck with her head a little more. However, she'd have to step outside her front door for me to mess with her, and the woman barely goes anywhere. Work and home are the sum of her existence, so tonight's excursion intrigued me.

And I want a front-row seat to the action.

My cell pings in my hand, pulling me out of my head as a call comes through. My finger hovers over the mute button until I see the caller ID. Shit timing, but there's no way I'm ignoring my little sister's call. She's only recently started talking to me again.

"Stay put," I tell Emilia, clicking my fingers at the bartender, gesturing at him to refill her drink.

I pick up the call. "Hey, Lil. I can't talk here. Give me a second to walk outside." Her response is drowned out by the noise as I push my way through the crowd toward the main entrance door.

"Are you okay?" I ask the second I'm outside where it's a lot quieter.

"I'm good," Lil replies. "Where are you?"

I nod at the bouncers by the door, walking off to the left and wedging myself into the shadowy corner of the building. I cradle the phone to my ear as I flatten my back against the wall. "At a club over on the west side."

"Mischief?" she asks.

"Yeah, that's the place."

"I've heard it's cool. All my friends have tried to get in, but they're, like, super strict."

"You will not be getting within one hundred miles of this place, Lil. It's definitely not suitable."

I was exposed to way worse at fifteen, but it's why I go out of my way to ensure Lil is protected from all that.

Mom may want nothing to do with me anymore, but that doesn't mean I've stopped caring. I have a team of guys watching my family twenty-four-seven, and they report to me daily. I don't want to worry Mom, but the elite threat hasn't evaporated with Dad's death or the FBI investigation. The new president is rebuilding the organization behind the front he presents to the authorities, and the danger is still ever present.

"Have you forgotten I live in Phoenix now?" Her dour tone vibrates down the line.

"Hardly, pumpkin. I miss your ugly face."

I can almost feel her smile down the line. "I miss your grumpy ass too. I hate this, Charlie. Isn't there anything you can do to make her talk to you?"

I sigh, rubbing at the sudden sharp pain in my chest. "I can't force her to forgive me."

"If I can forgive you, so can she," she blurts.

"I killed the man she loved, Lil. She might never forgive me."

Initial silence greets me. "You didn't kill Dad, Charlie." Her voice is low. "That murdering bastard did, and I hope he's rotting in hell."

"I made some bad decisions, and I'm living with the consequences now," I admit, kicking at a few loose stones on the sidewalk with the toe of my sneaker.

"She'll come around," Lil says. "She has to, because I hate this. I hate living with Aunt Marie and Uncle George. He smells like whiskey and cigarettes, and he creeps me out."

My spine turns rigid, and my entire body stiffens. "Has he—"

"He hasn't touched me," she says, cutting across me, "but he looks at me funny sometimes, and I don't like it."

That makes two of us. I make a mental note to call Knox, the guy in charge of the security detail in Phoenix, and request another check into Uncle George's background.

When Mom announced she was moving back to Arizona, to live with her older sister and her husband, and that she was taking Lil with her, I had full background checks conducted on both of them to make sure it was safe for my family to move there. Nothing out of the ordinary stuck out, but I want to take another look. I don't like the sound of this guy, and if he dares lay a finger on my sister, I will kill him with my bare hands. It wouldn't be the first time I've taken a life like that, and I wouldn't waste any sleep worrying about it.

Now, more than ever, I need to find a way of repairing my fractured relationship with Mom. I want them back home where they belong. Where I can keep a personal watch over them and ensure they are safe.

"Promise me you'll call me if anything happens," I say, as the sound of tinkling laughter greets my eardrums.

All the tiny hairs on the back of my neck stand up as I whip my head around, spotting Demi as she rounds the corner. She's linking arms with a girl with long purple hair, and they're both laughing at something the two guys behind them are saying.

A burning pain rips across my chest wall and a muscle ticks in my jaw, as I stare at the two inked, pierced degenerates, wondering which asshole is Demi's date, and what fucking hole he crawled out from, because she is always at work or at home, so when the hell did she have time to meet the prick?

"I promise," Lil says, dragging me back to the conversation. "If you promise to come visit soon."

Irritation prickles at my skin while I watch the small group joke around as they walk toward the entrance to the club. The guy with the dark faux hawk puts his hand on Demi's lower back as he steers her around a puddle on the ground, and a flare of something close to jealousy burns hotter in my chest. "I'll try my best, pumpkin. Look, I've got to go, but I'll call you tomorrow, 'kay?"

"Just one last thing!"

I drag my eyes up and down Demi's shapely form as she draws closer, lust stirring in my loins at the sight of her long, slim legs encased in skyscraper stilettos. Her lightweight jacket is open, revealing the short, tight black dress she's wearing. It clings to her body like a second skin, and my dick surges to life behind the crotch of my jeans.

"Charlie!"

Lil's shout brings me back into the moment. "I'm listening," I say, pressing back farther into the shadows in case Demi should happen to glance this way. "What were you saying?"

"Mom's freaking out over the invite. What should she do?"

I watch Demi disappear through the doors of the club as my sister's words register in my brain. "What invite?"

"Were you even listening to anything I said?" she huffs, and her pout carries down the line.

"I got distracted for that last part, but I've been listening, Lil."

"Mom got an invite to that elite ball."

I frown even though she can't see me. I haven't heard anything about any event, but if formal invites have been issued, I guess mine is sitting in the mountain of mail piled high on the kitchen table.

"I'll handle it," I reassure my sister, because there's no way in hell I want Mom anywhere near those sick bastards.

It's challenging though, because she's the widow of a man from a founding family, and as I haven't ascended to full status within the order yet, she is still duty bound to fulfill a role when called upon. My father successfully shielded her from the worst excesses of elitist life when he was alive, and I fully intend to continue keeping her away from that world.

If everything hadn't gone down the way it did in Wyoming, I'd be a full member now that I've graduated high school and I'm nineteen. But everything has been in limbo within the order since things were exposed, and I'm just waiting to find out what happens next. There's no doubt the new president will rectify things in due course.

"Tell her you've spoken to me and she's not to attend. I'll RSVP on her behalf with an excuse."

"Thanks, Charlie." Her relief is palpable.

"Anything, pumpkin. You know I've got your back."

"Call me tomorrow?" she asks.

"The second I wake," I promise, and we say our goodbyes. I slide the phone into the pocket of my jeans and make my way back inside the club.

I don't return to the bar, heading up the side stairway to the upper level, finding a perfect spot in front of the railing to people watch. I scan the room below, watching Emilia flirt with some guy at the bar with mild amusement, while my gaze continues roaming in search of my prey.

I find Demi, swaying her hips in time to the beat of the music, in the middle of the dance floor with her friend with the purple hair. Her limbs are elegant, her moves sophisticated, as she dances, oblivious to the attention she's garnering from various men surrounding her.

And I get it.

Demi is a beautiful woman, and she carries herself with grace. She's not one of those women who works hard to look sexy. She exudes sex appeal without even trying. And the fact she's blissfully unaware only adds to the attraction.

I know what Drew or any of the guys from my old circle would think if they saw her. That she's the fucking image of Abby with her long, wavy, dark hair, smoldering brown eyes, pouty lips, and slim frame. I can't deny they share similar physical traits—with the exception of her tits, because Mother Nature was generous with Demi in a way she wasn't with Abby, but it's more the shared characteristics I'm drawn to.

Guess I have a type.

Demi is comfortable in her own skin. She doesn't let anyone tell her how to be. And she's got backbone. She's a lot less mouthy than Abby, but when pushed, she knows how to push back.

I've tried to pinpoint exactly when Demi became a source of intrigue rather than irritation, and I think it's the fact she had ammunition to blackmail me and she chose not to.

I know her father needs constant care, thanks to his stroke, and I doubt there's much left of the generous severance package the company gave him, so I wouldn't have faulted her for exploiting the situation to her advantage, but she didn't do that.

If she had come to me, when I still believed I was married to Abby, and threatened to expose what happened Christmas night in the office, I would've written her a blank check on the spot. Because I was terrified for weeks that Abby would find out exactly what'd gone down that night and I would've done anything to stop it.

A grudging respect for Demi sprouted then although I hide that fact behind cruel words, sneering looks, and a generally abrasive manner.

Because it's better than the alternative—admitting to myself I've traded one obsession for another.

Chapter Four
Demi

The room tilts, and I grab on to Xena's arm to steady myself. Compared to what I used to drink on a night out, I have barely touched alcohol tonight, but I'm out of practice, and I'm definitely feeling a bit tipsy. But it's a happy buzz, and I haven't felt this relaxed in ages. "I'm gonna grab some water," I shout in my bestie's ear.

"I'll come with," she shouts back, but I shake my head, pushing her at her boyfriends. "Dance with your men. I'll be right over there." I point at an empty stool at the far end of the bar.

"We won't be long," she hollers, smacking a kiss to my temple.

I fight several pairs of grabby hands as I make my way toward the bar, giggling at the attention because it feels good to be desired, even if it's only superficial, and I have zero plans to indulge any man tonight.

I haul myself up on the stool, using the footrest to balance myself as I lean over the bar to snag the bartender's attention. I order a water, and I'm just about to sit back down when fingers brush against the back of my bare thigh. I swivel around, ready to punch the sleazy douche in the face, when I'm stopped short.

My eyes widen, and my mouth gapes open. "Isaac?!"

"Surprise, babe." My ex lifts me off the stool by the hips, reeling me into his strong embrace. The familiar scent of vanilla and sandalwood surrounds me, and I breathe him in, relaxing against him for a few seconds.

I ease back, keeping him at arm's length, as I peer up at him. "What are you doing here?"

"I came to wish you a happy birthday." He produces a slim, rectangular box from somewhere behind his body, handing it to me.

"Isaac. I can't accept this." I give it back at him. "We're not together anymore."

He shoves the gift into the back pocket of his jeans before tilting my chin up with his finger. Earnest blue eyes drill into mine. "That's something I was hoping we could fix."

My shocked gaze is locked on Isaac, so I don't notice the guy in the dark-fitted shirt until he slams into my ex, almost sending him tumbling to the floor. But Isaac has sharp reflexes, honed from years playing football with the Black Bears, and he grabs on to the edge of the counter in time, stopping his backward trajectory.

"What the hell is your problem?" he snaps as he straightens up.

"My bad," a familiar voice says, turning the blood in my veins to ice.

I jerk my head around, staring at Charlie with suspicion.

"Bumbling. Fancy running into you here," he says, wearing his trademark devilish grin. The one he usually puts on when he's gearing up to insult or humiliate me.

"You know this jerk?" Isaac wraps a protective arm around my shoulders, shooting daggers at Charlie.

"Not by choice," I admit. "He's my boss."

"Charles Barron the Third," Charlie says, introducing himself without invitation while glaring at my ex.

What a pompous ass.

"And I'd be careful what you say—unless you want Bumbling here to lose her job." He pins the full extent of his dark glare on me. "What a shame that would be."

"Why does he call you Bumbling?" Isaac asks, scrubbing his free hand along his smooth jawline, as he peers at Charlie, trying to figure out his game.

"He thinks he's amusing," I reply, deliberately ignoring Charlie even though every molecule of my body is finely attuned to his presence. "Bumbling as in bumbling idiot."

Isaac's jaw tenses, his back stiffens, and I know he's preparing to go in to battle on my behalf.

I place my hand on his chest. "Don't waste your energy. He's not worth it." My eyes sparkle with mirth, and I blame the beer on my next outburst. "Besides, I have my own pet names for him." I talk to Isaac, but my eyes are locked on Charlie's as the words leave my mouth. "Sometimes, he's Nimrod, per the ancient definition. Other times, he's pencil dick." I mock smile at Charlie, annoyed when his lips curve up at the corners. The guy must have a stone heart because nothing ever penetrates that hard shell.

He smirks. "So, you think I'm a tyrannical leader with a long, thin dick which is interesting because you may well be right on the first, but we both know the second is a *big, fat lie.*"

I spot the evil glint in his eye as he eyeballs my ex, and I clamp my hand down over his mouth before he can spill the beans on our night together. Not that it really matters. Isaac and I had broken up by then, and despite what he just said to me, we're not getting back together.

Still, I spent three years of my life with Isaac, and there was a time I thought he was the one.

What he thinks of me matters.

"Charles." A willowy blonde sidles up to Charlie, circling her slender arm around his back, while peering up at him with a confused expression on her face.

A flash of annoyance ghosts over Charlie's face, but it's so fleeting I'm not sure my drunken mind didn't conjure it up.

"Darling." Charlie smiles adoringly at the woman as he envelops her in his arms. "I'm sorry I was gone so long, but I just bumped into the help, and I felt obligated to say hello."

My hackles are instantly raised. It's one thing for him to insult me in the confines of his office and quite another to insult me with an audience.

"Consider your obligation fulfilled, *Charles*." I enunciate the word on purpose, knowing he'll hate it because I've watched him bristle time and time again when some of the older members of staff call him that.

I guess it reminds him of his father.

At any other time, I would never stoop so low, but my claws are out, and it's every man, and woman, for themselves. "I'm contractually bound to deal with you during the work week, but I'm under no legal compulsion to stomach your disgusting company outside of the office, so do us both a favor and fuck the hell off."

Heat rolls off Charlie in deadly waves, knocking me off kilter. He tightens his grip on his date as he drills me with a look that promises a world of pain for daring to challenge him in public.

Well, fuck him.

He can't dictate to me what I do and say outside working hours.

"Careful, Bumbling." His dark voice slashes at my alcohol-fueled confidence, making large dents in it. "I'll think you'll find, if you read the small print of your contract, that you represent the business at all times and any conduct unbecoming of a company employee can result in disciplinary action."

The blonde smirks, clearly enjoying the show, and I scowl at her as Isaac opens his mouth, to defend me, no doubt. I send him a subtle headshake, and he clamps his lips shut.

"Insubordination of the president of the company, irrespective of where or when it takes place, is strictly forbidden. Check the disciplinary rules if you don't believe me." He swipes his finger along the screen of his cell, thrusting it at me.

I refuse to take it or this bullshit charade. "Just go away, Charlie."

His green eyes turn darker. "Apologize and I'll let this pass."

I crank out a laugh. "Yeah, I don't think so." I turn to Isaac. "Are you ready to leave?"

"I was ready the instant this asshole stuck his nose into our business," he replies, taking my elbow and steering me away.

But Charlie grabs hold of my other arm, drawing me back. "Think of how badly you need this job, Demi," he whispers in my ear, and I hate the shudder that ripples through my body as his warm breath swirls around me. "Who'll pay the medical bills if you're out of work?"

My fists clench into balls at his veiled threat. He's never indicated he knew anything about my personal life, but I should've known he'd pry into my affairs. It's not exactly a secret around the office, because most people I work with knew my dad, but Charlie has never once brought him up to me.

"Do. Not. Bring. My. father. Into this." I grind my teeth down as anger radiates through ever cell in my body.

"Drop to your knees, kiss my feet, and we'll call it even."

I don't need to think about it. Not even for one second.

Hell will freeze over before I kiss that asshole's feet or bow down to him in any way. "Get fucked, Charlie."

He barks out a dry laugh. "Oh, I fully intend to." He shoots a wickedly carnal look at the blonde hanging off his arm, and most every woman in the vicinity swoons because they've all clearly got shit for brains.

"Darling. I need you now," she says, rubbing her lithe body up against his as she palms his crotch, uncaring who sees.

"Let's go," Isaac hisses, taking my hand in his large, warm palm.

"Enjoy my sloppy seconds," Charlie says, projecting his voice so everyone around us can hear. "She's not even that good of a lay, but if you're that desperate, go for it."

My hand is raised before I've even processed the motion, and I slap him firmly across one cheek, my entire body thrumming with anger. "How dare you." I push myself all up in his face, watching out of the corner of my eye as Bo and Leo materialize from the dance floor, holding Isaac back, attempting to talk him out of going postal on Charlie's ass.

Charlie's eyes are cold and devoid of emotion as he takes hold of the blonde's hand while staring at me. "Thank you, Bumbling, for finally giving me what I've wanted since that night."

He leans down close to my face, and Isaac shouts and squirms as the guys struggle to hold him at bay. "Your ass on a platter." His lips curl into a sneer. "Don't bother showing up on Monday. You can collect your termination papers from the human resources department." He storms off, towing the blonde, teetering on high heels, behind him.

"Fuck." I slap a hand against my forehead. "What the hell have I done?"

"He can't fire you," Bo says, when we're back at the apartment he shares with Xena and Leo.

"Eh, not to be the harbinger of doom, but he probably can," Leo says, handing me a vodka shot.

"Babe. We're supposed to be cheering her up," Xena protests, warning Leo to back down with her eyes.

"Leo is right." The asshole was too. Now that I'm sober-ish, I'm seeing things in a different light. "It *is* against company policy to do or say anything which might bring the company into disrepute. I'm pretty sure slapping the president, the current majority shareholder of the business, in public, falls into that category."

"From what you've said, he's been verbally abusive to you since he took over that role. Maybe, if you lodge a countercomplaint against him, it will go away," Isaac says, rubbing my arm in a gesture I used to find comforting.

I wiggle my arm out from under him, pretending I don't see his puzzled, hurt expression. "I'm pretty sure it's too late for that. If I bring it up now, it'll look like I'm trying to fabricate an argument not to fire me." I knock back my vodka shot, relishing the sharp taste as it glides down my throat. "I should've just bitten my tongue. God knows, I've had enough practice around him."

"He can't get away with this," Isaac huffs, indignant on my behalf. "He's a fucking bully, and there are laws against that." He runs his hands through his sandy-blond hair in a clear show of agitation.

"Maybe it's a blessing in disguise," Xena says, topping up my shot glass. "He's made your life hell."

"And you have almost a year's experience under your belt now," Bo adds. "That will look great on your résumé. I'm sure you'll pick up work elsewhere."

Maybe, I'll apply for a job at Manning Motors.

That'd be sure to piss Charlie off.

I shrug. "Maybe." *Who knows, perhaps my friends are right and it's the best thing to happen, so why do I feel so ill at the thought of leaving?*

The others discreetly disappear, giving Isaac and me some time alone to talk. Xena has offered him her couch for the night, because I've already got dibs on the guest bedroom.

"I'm sorry you've been dealing with all that shit on your own," Isaac says, handing me a cup of chamomile tea.

I pull the blanket off the back of the couch, draping it over my bare legs and feet. "It hasn't been so bad. The job is actually more interesting than I thought it'd be."

"But it's not accounting."

"No." I blow on the top of the cup, taking a tentative sip of the hot tea. "But it probably would've led to a job in the finance department."

"How's your dad?" he asks, purposely switching the subject.

"He's just been diagnosed with stage four stomach cancer."

"Shit. I'm sorry, baby." He scoots closer, attempting to pull me into his arms, but I shuck him off.

"Don't, Isaac. And I'm not your baby anymore."

"You're pissed."

I turn to face him.

He's biting on his lower lip and running his hands through his hair. "I know I went a bit crazy these past few months, but you left me, and I was distraught." He leans forward, stabbing me with a sincere look. "None of the girls I was with meant anything." He reaches for my hand, but I shake my head, and he pulls back. "You're the only woman I've ever loved."

"You have a funny way of showing it," I say, in between sipping my tea.

The truth is, I *was* a little hurt when my ex-roommate and

best friend told me about Isaac's new manwhore rep around campus but not nearly as hurt as I should've been. It became obvious, very quickly, that what Isaac and I shared was over long before I broke things off. Something I did because trying to maintain a long-distance relationship, as well as working full-time, and caring for my disabled father, would never have worked out.

Even though it killed me back then, I knew ending things was the best thing for both of us.

And I haven't regretted my decision, because the truth is, I haven't missed him.

Not in the way I should.

"You didn't reach out to me, at all, after I left UMaine. Not even to inquire after Dad." That disappointed me above everything, because Isaac and I were great friends before we became more, and I thought he might at least have checked in on me from time to time.

"I wanted to, but you hurt me."

I stare at him incredulously, wondering where the sweet, considerate guy I fell for has disappeared to.

I guess I'm not the only one who's changed.

"Isaac. My dad had a stroke. He almost died. He was paralyzed and kicked out of his job. It's not like I made a conscious choice to break up with you, but it was the only decision that made sense." I shake my head in disgust. "And from what I've heard, it seems like you didn't have much difficulty moving on."

He, at least, has the decency to look ashamed.

Silence engulfs us for a few minutes.

"Did you really hook up with that jerk?" he asks, and I'm tempted to hit him. *After everything I just said, that's what he wants to say to me?*

"It was one time. When I had temporary brain failure," I

quip, because that's the only way I can reconcile the epic mistake in my head.

"Have you dated?" he asks, continuing to pry.

Man, he really is clueless. "I barely have time to breathe most days, let alone date, Isaac."

"I'm sorry I abandoned you. That was insensitive and hurtful of me." He moves in closer. "But I'm here now. I want to be here for you if you'll let me make it up to you." Sincerity oozes from his pores, and I know he means it, but he's got blinders on.

"I forgive you, Isaac, and I appreciate you saying that, and coming to see me, but what we have is in the past, and it's time you forgot about me. I will always cherish the time we shared, but we're not right for one another."

His chest heaves as he stares at me. "Is it him?"

My jaw trails to the floor. "Are you serious right now? Did you not see what went down earlier?"

"I saw *exactly* what went down earlier," he retorts, in a clipped tone, standing up and grabbing his jacket from the back of the chair. "I don't think I'm the one who has issues seeing things clearly." He leans down, pressing a kiss to my cheek. "He's not good enough for you, Demi. And I've seen his type before. He'll only use you up and then toss you aside. You're worth way more than that."

Yes, I am.

I watch him walk out of Xena's apartment and out of my life for good.

I also know I'm better than my behavior tonight. *But the million-dollar question is, what am I going to do about this new mess I find myself in?*

Chapter Five
Charlie

I wake Sunday morning with a monster hangover, thanks to the half bottle of JD I poured down my throat when I got home. I roll over in my bed, groaning as I stretch my arm out, feeling along the top of my bedside table for my cell. Finding it, I turn over and prop myself up with some pillows against the headboard.

I stay in bed as I scroll through my inbox. Most are work emails, and I've got a couple of missed calls from some guys I know from Parkhurst. I ignore the angry texts from Emilia, deleting and blocking her number so I don't have to deal with her shit ever again.

She was *not* impressed when I dropped her home and refused to come in. I had zero interest in screwing her after what went down at the club. Instead, I jerked off in the shower to thoughts of Demi's rage-filled eyes, coming violently against the tile wall.

After I call Lil, I pull on some sweats and pad downstairs in my bare feet. Ghosts of the past follow me as I traipse into the kitchen, and I remember noisy mornings, filled with conversation and laughter, Mom's homemade honey and apple muffins, and Dad's freshly squeezed orange juice.

I plant my hands on the edge of the sink, staring absently out the window at the massive gardens spanning the rear of the vast property, wondering how it all went so wrong.

I squeeze my eyes shut, warding off further memories, and the painful ache in my chest serves as a constant reminder of everything I've lost.

After a few minutes, I force my tired body to move, switching the Keurig on and pouring a bowl of granola. The only sound in the room is a crunching noise as I shovel spoonsful of cereal in my mouth.

There are a lot of things I hate about my life now, but the constant silence is the thing I hate most. My desolation is reflected in the hollow echo bouncing off the walls, and I can't stand it any longer.

Jumping up, I storm into the laundry room, grabbing my sneakers. I lace them tight and exit the house via the rear side door, jogging to the running track that skims the perimeter of the woodland at the far side of our garden.

I only have my depressive thoughts for company as I attempt to outrun my demons, and I push my body hard while I'm silently screaming inside.

I arrive back at the house sometime later, dripping in sweat and breathless, but at least, I feel more alive, and the brisk morning air has chased some of the cobwebs from my throbbing head.

I grab a quick shower, pop a couple of pain pills, and head down to my home office to complete an assignment due this week. I pass by the locked door of my father's study with the usual lump in my throat. Neither Mom nor I could stomach going in there after he died, so we locked it up and threw away the key.

After I complete the assignment, I pull up the app on my cell, checking on Demi's whereabouts. She's only a half mile from home, and I'm tempted to get in my car, drive over there, and tell her to forget about last night, but I manage to talk myself out of it.

Her leaving the office is the best option for both of us, because nothing good can come from this obsession.

Abby was the last woman I fixated on, and everyone knows how badly that turned out.

She might not believe it, but Demi leaving Barron Banking and Financial Investment Services is the best way of keeping her safe.

***

Knox calls me bright and early on Monday morning to confirm he's allocated a man to follow Uncle George and he's personally going to investigate him. I tell him to keep me updated and end the call, climbing into the back seat of my chauffeur-driven car and instructing the driver to take me to the office instead of campus. I want to be there when Demi arrives, so I can see what she does. I also want to work my way through the mountain of unopened mail, so I've purposely chosen not to drive myself today.

Arthur Fleming, the CEO, is the only other person present on the executive floor when I arrive. The office doesn't officially open for another couple hours, so it's not unusual it's this quiet.

"No classes today?" he inquires when I enter the small kitchenette.

"I need to catch up on a few things here that were more urgent," I say, and it's not really a lie.

"Have you met with Simon Reed yet?" He takes his coffee

and leans back against the counter, determined to make small talk.

"The meeting is set for next week." I fix my coffee, giving him my back.

It's not that I don't like the guy.

I like him well enough.

But there's a natural competitive rivalry between us.

Technically, Arthur's on borrowed time, because the agreement Dad made with him was that I will take the CEO role, the pole position within the firm, once I graduate with my degree and provided I've successfully passed all stages of the training plan he left in place for me.

When Dad first died, I assumed I would be installed as CEO immediately. But Dad had covered all his bases, leaving clear instructions that if he died before I graduated Rydeville University, I was to continue my education and work part-time in the company as president, the second-most senior role and a position that gives me access to every facet of the company while I learn the ropes.

The logical part of my brain concurs it's a smart plan. The arrogant side of my personality calls bullshit on the need for it. I'm already proving to be a fast learner and a natural leader, and my appetite for knowledge is above reproach. I hate that I'm wasting my mornings on campus, because that's exactly what it feels like to me. Parkhurst prepared us well for assuming responsibility within our family businesses, and I've already covered a lot of ground. But I have no choice unless I want to relinquish my control over the business by failing to deliver on Dad's successor planning.

"I'd like to sit in on the meeting," Arthur says, as I add creamer to my coffee.

"I've got it covered." I dare him to challenge me with a sharp look.

He purses his lips before nodding. "As you wish. I look forward to reading your report. I've heard some favorable things about him, and if the system he's developed is as good as it claims to be, we need to be all over it. I'd like to tie him down to an exclusive contract so he can't take it elsewhere."

"If it's suitable and it offers efficiencies and cost savings, we'll make him an offer he can't refuse," I agree.

We end our conversation, heading to our respective offices, and I leave my door ajar, settling in behind my desk to wait for my PA to arrive.

Demi shows up forty-five minutes before official opening time, and I watch her hang up her coat and power up her computer like a sneaky Peeping Tom. She hasn't noticed my door is slightly open. She hasn't even glanced this way. Because she presumes I'm at college, like usual.

She removes some files from her desk drawer, pops on her headphones, and begins typing away.

My lips twitch as I wonder if this is her game plan. If she's going to pretend like nothing happened.

If she wants me to make the first move, I'm down with that. I pick up my desk phone and press the button to summon her.

Startled, she visibly jumps in her seat, and I watch her gaze grow wide as she stares at the phone like it's going to grow teeth and bite her. An involuntary grin spreads across my mouth as her head jerks up in the direction of my office. Her face pales when she spots me, and I mentally rub my hands in glee.

I'm starting to see why Anderson enjoyed playing the asshole with Abby. Although, in his case, there was minimal acting involved. Because the guy's a bona fide douche.

I curl my fingers at her in a come hither gesture, never taking my eyes off her as she stands, smoothing a hand down the front of her wrinkled black pencil skirt. She snatches her notepad and pen, and I examine every inch of her as she walks toward me, noticing how badly she's trying to hide her fear. She holds her head up high as she enters my office.

"Shut the door," I command, swiveling in my chair as I tap my Montblanc pen on the top of my desk.

Her hands are shaking as she shuts the door, but she quickly composes herself, tipping her chin up and fixing me with a determined look. She walks to my desk, and I point at one of the empty chairs in front of it with my pen. "Sit."

She slides onto the chair, crossing one slim leg over the other, and I catch a glimpse of the lacy top of her stockings. My cock jerks behind my zipper, and I silently caution the beast to calm down.

"What do you need, Mr. Barron?" she asks, adopting the formal tone she uses in the office.

"An explanation, Ms. Alexander." I drill her with a dark look. "I believe I made myself perfectly clear Saturday night."

She puts her notepad down on her lap, clasping her hands on top of it. "I was hoping we could agree to put that incident behind us. We'd both been drinking, and I'm sure we said things we didn't mean."

I lean forward in my chair, placing my pen down. I rest my elbows on the desk and stare at her. She's wearing her dark hair up in an elegant chignon, exposing the delicate column of her slender neck. Her pretty lips are coated in a light layer of gloss, and her gorgeous big, brown eyes are rimmed by a layer of long, fat lashes.

She truly has the most stunning face.

Perfectly symmetrical in its beauty.

If she was taller, I bet every modeling agency in town would be beating a path to her door.

My gaze drops to her mouth, and an image of her plump lips wrapped around my cock has me straining painfully in my pants.

I force myself to focus. "Don't presume to put words in my mouth. I assure you, I was perfectly sober," I lie.

Her tongue darts out, wetting her lips, and my eyes are like heat-seeking missiles tracking the movement.

"I apologize for my behavior," she says, her voice ringing out loud and confidently. She stares me directly in the face, and her solemn expression conveys the truth of her words. "It was disrespectful, completely beneath me, and I promise you nothing like that will ever happen again."

I quirk a brow. "Am I expected to take you at your word?"

She's momentarily flustered. "Yes. You've worked with me long enough to know I'm reliable. If I tell you I'll do something, I do it."

That's true. I doubt being a personal assistant is her dream job, but I can't deny her commitment. She throws herself into every task with professionalism and enthusiasm, and I haven't made it easy on her.

But she never complains.

She just gets on with things.

I know Arthur believes she has untapped potential, and she's popular with the other secretaries and assistants.

Demi is a good girl.

Far too good for someone like me.

Which is why she really should keep her distance, because I'm not convinced I have the tenacity to stay away from her for much longer.

"And if I tell you that's not good enough. That you crossed a line you can't come back from, what would you say?" Adrenaline races through my veins at the sheer panic etched upon her beautiful face.

"Please, Charlie. You know why I need this job."

"This isn't a charity. Save your sob story because that truly is beneath you." I'm being an asshole on purpose, because I want to poke the beast.

Fire blazes in her eyes, and her legendary backbone makes an appearance. Demi's natural inclination is to appease, and she doesn't court conflict. But that doesn't mean she's a pushover. When challenged, she can more than hold her own. For months, I've pushed and pushed her, and she is well capable of fighting back.

I silently encourage her to go on.

"I have other stories I could tell," she says, sitting up straighter. The vein in her neck pulses as she grows more animated. "I think the media would love to hear how the new president is nothing more than a bully who gets off on abusing and belittling his PA. Or how a company, who prides itself on its traditional family image, tossed a loyal employee to the curb the minute he was no longer of any use to them. I'm betting they would pay handsomely for such a story."

I wonder if she actually has the balls to do it. I think if I pushed hard enough, she would. But that's a nightmare the PR people would not thank me for, and I'm still the new guy at the top, so deliberately ruffling feathers would not be intelligent.

"You signed a nondisclosure agreement, as did your father when he accepted our severance package. No one forced either of you to sign." I stand and walk around the desk, towering over her on purpose. "You breathe one derogatory word about me, or the company, and we will take legal action. You won't have a penny to your name by the time we're done." It's not an idle threat. I will go all out to protect what is mine.

"You can't threaten me!" She rises, waving her finger in my face. "I'll file a complaint with the ACLU. There are laws to protect employees who are victimized in the workplace, NDA or not!"

A red stain creeps up her neck and onto her cheeks, and

I'm quite partial to that aggressive, flushed look on her face. My cock agrees, aching against my zipper.

Visions of Demi handcuffed to my bed, on all fours, with her reddened ass sticking up in the air, dance across my mind's eye, turning my erection rock hard.

I can't remember the last time I was this hot for a woman.

If ever.

If she looks down, there will be no disguising how much this turns me on.

How much *she* turns me on.

This is the most fun I've had in ages, and I've got zero desire to dial down my assholishness.

I push into her personal space, and she stumbles back, falling into the chair. I plant my hands on either side of her, gripping the armrests, as I lean my face super close to hers. I angle my head, pressing my mouth to her ear. My warm breath fans across her delicate skin, raising tiny goose bumps along her sensitive flesh. I remember how responsive she was to my touch, and the craving to touch her again is almost too much.

"Were you victimized when you lowered your wet pussy down on my throbbing cock?" I whisper in her ear. "Or when you scraped your nails up and down my back, leaving marks?" I run my nose up the column of her neck, and I'm dangerously close to losing control.

Her body trembles underneath me, and she's holding herself rigidly still, fighting this crazy desire pulsing between us.

"Answer me," I snap before pressing my mouth to the underside of her jaw.

A tiny whimper flies out of her mouth. "I'm not referring to that, and you know it."

"There is an easy way to settle this," I say, clasping hold of her wrist. "If this job means that much to you, I can let your disgraceful behavior pass if your apology is sincere enough."

"It is!" she cries, lifting her eyes and staring at me.

I push off the chair and straighten up, leveling her with a heated stare that comes from pure, visceral need. "Prove it."

Her eyes narrow suspiciously but she doesn't shy away. "How?"

"Unzip my pants, get on your knees, and suck me off. Do a good job, and I'll forget Saturday night ever existed."

Chapter Six
Demi

"You can't be serious?" My voice elevates a few octaves as panic swaddles me.

"As a heart attack," he coolly replies. His dark gaze challenges me, but I can't figure out if it's a test. *Does he want me to obey or fight him on it?*

I stand, and our chests brush in the process, sending a wave of heat flooding through me. Ignoring my cursed libido, I glare at him. "I'm not blowing you. That is unethical, illegal, and downright disgusting."

He smirks, and the urge to slap him again is riding me hard.

"Let's not pretend, Demi." He places his thumb on my neck, just underneath my jawline, right in the spot where my pulse is jumping like crazy. "There would be nothing disgusting about it, and we both know it."

He cocks his head to the side as his thumb swipes back and forth across my overly sensitive flesh. "I know you're a good girl, Demi. Everyone can see that." He leans in close to my face, lining his lips up with mine, keeping scant distance between us.

At this proximity, his spicy, woodsy scent assaults me, holding me prisoner, ensuring I can't move a muscle.

"But I also know you're a naughty, dirty girl." He presses a kiss to the corner of my mouth. "And I'm guessing that side of you hasn't been explored." He trails his hand up the side of my thigh, over my skirt, but I still feel his touch skin-deep. "I know you want to do it, dirty girl. You want to sink to your knees and let me fuck your mouth until you're gagging and choking and enjoying every mouthwatering moment." He grips my hip hard, and I gasp, the pain sending a torrent of heat to my core.

A switch flicks in my brain, and I shove at his chest, pushing him back a couple steps. "You know nothing, Mr. Barron. I'm not some cheap whore you can manipulate. I have more self-respect." A thought pops into my head, and I blurt it out before I can stop myself. "I hear Manning Motors is recruiting," I lie. "Perhaps I'll send them my resume." It's a deliberate punch to the gut, because Manning Motors is the company owned by Abby's family. If my research is correct, Abby works there part-time alongside her twin brother, Drew.

The change in Charlie's temperament is swift, fierce, and borderline concerning. I barely have time to register the fury in his eyes before his hands wrap around my throat and he pushes me across the room, slamming my back against the wall beside the door.

"You know nothing, Ms. Alexander, or you'd know better than to go there."

My heart is pounding in my chest, and every nerve ending in my body is on high alert. Blood rushes to my head, and my panties are soaked with need as adrenaline surges through my body. Charlie presses the length of his body against me, and I feel his hard erection nudge against my stomach as he strokes my neck with his thumbs. His fingers are still wrapped around my throat, and I'm weirdly aroused where a sane woman would be scared out of her freaking mind. But Charlie's harsh touch awakens dark desires hidden deep inside me, and I don't want to stop this.

He glares at me as his lips descend, slamming down on mine with brutal force. His hands leave my throat, cradling the nape of my neck firmly as he destroys my mouth with a slew of violent kisses. I know I should push him away, but my body is way too invested, and I'm kissing him back with the same fervor, my hands gripping his waist and holding him flush to my body so I can feel every inch of his ripped form.

He pushes his tongue into my mouth, and I groan as I writhe against him, my body wired and primed to explode.

He kisses me like he's eating me. Tasting, biting, and sucking, and I'm clawing at him, desperate for more, unwilling to let this end. His hand around my neck is possessive as he angles my head, directing the kiss, diving even deeper, while rocking his hips against my pelvis, his need clearly as severe as my own.

Without warning, he rips his mouth from mine, unbuckles his belt and lets his pants fall to his ankles. He drills me with a look that's so intense I feel stripped naked. "Wrap your lips around my cock, baby. I need to feel your hot mouth on me."

I open my mouth, to say what I'm not sure, but he shakes his head, rubbing his thumb along my bruised lower lip. "Don't fight it. We both want this."

I'm clearly insane, or high on lust, because I push off the wall, grab the band of his boxers, and shove them down his muscular thighs, freeing his impressive cock. It springs up, long, thick, and inviting, and I wet my lips in anticipation, brushing my thumb along the bead of precum covering his crown. Charlie pushes on my shoulders, forcing me to the ground. I glare at him as I settle on my knees. He grins. "Open your mouth, baby, and suck my cock."

I grab hold of his left thigh to steady myself before taking him into my mouth.

He's an impatient bastard, thrusting forward immediately, and I gag as he hits the back of my throat. Tears leak out of my eyes as I force my mouth wider to accommodate him. He starts moving in and out as I slide my lips up and down his hard length. With my free hand, I grip the base of his cock and start pumping him aggressively.

He throws back his head, groaning as I hit my stride, sucking him harder and harder, while I frantically pump his shaft.

"Fuck, yes, baby. Just like that."

He jabs his hips forward as he grabs hold of the back of my head, holding me in place. Then, he fucks my mouth with no consideration for me, and I work in tandem with his movements, ignoring the tears streaming from my eyes and the gagging sensation each time he hits the back of my throat.

It's filthy, degrading, and seriously fucking hot, and I suck him off with determination, wanting his cum filing my mouth.

He growls low, and his entire body tenses, and that's the only warning I get as he shoots warm, salty cum straight down my throat. He continues pulsing and jerking inside me until I've swallowed every last drop. Pulling out, he yanks his pants up before lifting me up by the hips and throwing me over his shoulder.

Before I can protest, he drapes me across the width of his desk, shoving papers aside and bunching my skirt up to my waist. A shrill tear echoes through the electrically charged air as he rips my lace panties into shreds.

My chest heaves, and liquid warmth rushes my core when he nudges my thighs aside, parting the folds of my pussy and diving in with his seductive lips.

"Oh my God." I stretch my arms up over my head, grabbing

the edge of the desk to steady myself as my boss works me into a frenzy in record time with his magical fingers and tongue. When he places his thumb against the crack of my ass and pushes it in a little, I shatter explosively, biting down hard on my lip and drawing blood as I bottle up the scream dying to let loose.

I don't move when he withdraws, lying stretched across his desk with floppy limbs that feel incapable of working. My heart thumps behind my rib cage as I attempt to steady my breathing and recalibrate my brain.

What the hell have I done?

I find the strength to sit up and pull my skirt down, covering myself as I stare at the torn strips of my panties littering the floor around Charlie's desk. I lift my head, and my gaze locks on his.

We stare silently at one another, electricity fizzing in the air along with so many unspoken sentiments. His stoic mask is in place, and I can't get a read on him until he clears his throat abruptly. "Grab your shit and get back to your desk," he says in that robotic tone he uses on me sometimes. He looks away, tucking himself properly behind his pants and tightening his belt in place.

His dismissal isn't all that strange, but it's hurtful in the extreme. He is so closed off. So cold after something so wickedly intimate, and I'm not the kind of girl who lets a guy do that and then reject her.

Aren't you? my vicious inner voice taunts, because it's not like this is the first time I've let him use me.

I want to say something, anything, but a messy ball of emotion clogs my throat, blocking any form of communication. I slide off the desk, crouching down and collecting the remnants of my panties. I round his desk, tossing the scraps in the trash can, fighting to maintain what little dignity I have left.

Shame and hurt bubble inside me as I reach for my notepad and pen.

"Demi."

I look up as he steps toward me, his eyes searching mine.

"What?" I croak.

His hypnotic green eyes bore into mine, and for a second, emotion flashes across his features, disappearing quickly when he shuts it down. "Here." He hands me my notepad and pen, averting his eyes, and I know he's chickened out of whatever he was going to say.

Coward. I think it, but I don't say it. I don't say anything, and neither does he as I walk across the room and exit his office, praying no one is there to see my walk of shame.

After I've fixed my hair and makeup in the employee bathroom, I return to my desk, trying to ignore the fact I'm now wearing no underwear. Thank fuck, no one was around to bear witness to my mistake. I seem to be fond of making those kinds of mistakes around that man, and it's got to stop.

My hands are shaking as I put my headphones on, returning to the report I was starting before Charlie called me in to his office.

I try to focus on listening to the audio notes, but I'm distracted, wondering what the hell is going on between him and me. And whether this means my job is safe. I should, at least, have asked him that. But I was embarrassed at how easily I succumbed to his charms, and I just wanted to get out of there.

I really need to get laid.

Maybe then, I won't be putty in his manipulative hands.

My embarrassment soon turns to anger, and I pound my fingers over the keys as my rage seethes under the surface.

How dare he treat me like that!

I wonder if he was imagining I was *her* again. *When he*

closed his eyes and my lips were wrapped around his dick, was he visualizing Abby sucking him off, and when he was eating me out, was it her pussy he was tasting?

Ugh. I rip the headset off my ears and stand, needing to walk off the storm brewing inside me. I grab my coat and spin around, knocking into someone holding a carry out tray. I watch in horror as the tray drops to the floor, spilling two cups of steaming coffee all over the new gray carpet. "Shit."

"At least, it didn't spill on us," an amused feminine voice says.

I lift my head up, and my horror elevates to coronary-inducing territory as I stare into the warm brown eyes of Charlie's ex.

Chapter Seven
Demi

She blinks excessively as her gaze roams my face, her eyes widening as she mentally ticks off all the similarities. She's never been here before, at least not while I've been working here, so I'm guessing she has no clue who I am or that I'm practically her doppelgänger.

"I'm so sorry," I blurt, finally finding my voice and my place. "I'll clean up this mess and get some replacement coffees."

"It was an accident, and that's not necessary." She glances at Charlie's closed office door. "It was a peace offering, but I probably won't be here long enough for you to bring fresh coffee." She thrusts out her hand. "I'm Abby. A friend of Charlie's, eh, Mr. Barron," she adds, smiling.

I shake her hand in a bit of a daze. "I'm Demi. Mr. Barron's assistant."

"Nice to meet you, Demi. I was hoping to surprise Charlie. Is he free now?"

Margaret Ann scurries past me, eyes wide, holding a wad of paper towels and a bowl of water as she lowers to the floor.

"He's free," I confirm, not needing to check his schedule. I never schedule anything for the mornings because he's usually at college. "Let me announce you."

I shoot Margaret Ann a grateful look as I walk to Charlie's door and knock briefly before opening it. "Mrs. Anderson is here to see you," I say in a clipped voice, stepping aside to let Abby enter. Charlie hops up out of his chair, running a hand through his dark hair in a nervous tell.

Abby's brows knit together as she glances at me, and I realize my fuckup. "Thanks, Demi. And sorry about the mess. I'd help you clean up, but Charlie would probably scale the side of the building in a bid to get away from me, and I came here today determined to say what I need to say."

"It's fine, and it's no trouble."

Charlie's fearful gaze bounces between us, and awkward tension crackles in the air. Abby's frown deepens as she looks at him and then me. Slowly, she walks toward him while I'm rooted to the spot.

"That will be all, Ms. Alexander," Charlie says, shooing me with a flick of his hand like I'm an annoying insect.

Hurt blossoms in my chest.

"Close the door, and I'm not to be disturbed."

I nod, shutting the door with more force than necessary. Splintering pain slams into me, but I force it to one side, dropping down beside Margaret Ann, Mr. Fleming's PA, to help clean up the mess.

"That's her," she whispers as we mop up the bitter liquid with towels. "The ex-wife."

"He wasn't actually legally married to her," I say, recalling the research I conducted online many months ago.

When Charlie dropped the wife bombshell on me Christmas night, I was hurt, enraged, and disgusted.

But I was also curious.

Because, if he was newly married, why the hell wasn't his wife consoling him over his father's death? And why wasn't he having sex with her instead of me? It didn't add up, so I went online because Google is always a reliable friend. I discovered a press release confirming he had indeed married Abigail Hearst-Manning earlier that day.

To say I was shocked when I pulled up a picture of her is an understatement. The striking resemblance between us is eerie, and though I know it's not possible, if someone said we were long-lost twins, I'd have a hard time not believing it.

"It might not have been legal, but they lived together as husband and wife for a while," she says, as we continue cleaning.

Thanks so much for the reminder.

I keep my eyes focused on the task at hand for fear my emotion will betray me, vigorously scrubbing at the stain on the carpet.

I was a basket case for weeks after I had sex with Charlie, fearing his new bride would show up at any time and see the truth written all over my face. The office was awash with gossip over his sudden marriage to the Manning Motors heiress, and it's a wonder I had any nails left during that time.

Then the news broke about what happened in Wyoming. Where the FBI raided a conference at Parkhurst, a private pharmaceutical and medical corporation servicing high-end, wealthy clients, which was a front for a supposed elitist organization comprised of powerful members from business and government.

Charlie had been in attendance, and so had Abby and her brother and her legally-wed husband—Kaiden Anderson.

A bomb had detonated at the conference, and people had died. Several others were injured. But that was only the tip of the iceberg. Tons of stuff emerged about illegal activities the organization was involved in. It was a global scandal and a PR nightmare for my employer. They had to issue press release after press release denying any involvement with Parkhurst or the elite.

Charlie wasn't around in the initial aftermath, because he was injured in the explosion. He was in the hospital for a while, and then, he spent a few weeks working from home while he recuperated.

It was around that time Arthur Fleming pulled everyone aside and explained that Charlie was no longer married, that he hadn't actually ever been married, and not to broach the subject with him, as it was a source of discomfort and embarrassment. So, when Charlie returned, no one mentioned Abby, and it wasn't long before Charlie resumed his manwhore lifestyle and his bullying treatment of me.

I was intrigued about his situation with Abby though, especially when a pretty wedding invitation arrived at the end of July. Abby and Kaiden were holding a formal wedding reception, and they'd invited him. I wanted to see his reaction, so I placed it on top of his mail that day, watching as his entire face turned red when he opened it. He immediately tore it up, letting the ragged pieces of paper flutter to the floor while he stomped out of the office, not to be seen for several days.

That told me a lot.

I don't know about Abby, but Charlie was definitely in love with her.

I suspect he probably still is.

And that thought does nothing to help my current mood.

I call the maintenance department when I return to my desk, asking them to send someone up because Margaret Ann and I have done everything we can, but the stain still lingers.

Then, I walk to the kitchenette, make a pot of coffee, and

load a tray with it, some cups, creamer, sugar, and some oatmeal cookies.

Charlie hates those cookies, preferring the chocolate ones, but he's not in my good books right now.

He's lucky I don't lace his coffee with poison.

I rap once on the door before entering without invitation. I almost drop the tray at the sight that awaits me.

Abby is draped over Charlie in an intimate gesture that equally boils my blood and lays siege to my vulnerable heart. Her butt is propped against the front of Charlie's desk and she's leaning over him, her face all up in his, her arm on his shoulder, peering at him with an obvious mix of concern and adoration.

"Sorry to interrupt," I snap, stalking across the room. "I just thought you might like some coffee." *Over your head*, my gnarly inner voice says, as I slap the tray down, rattling the cups and spilling some coffee from the pot.

Charlie wears his usual cold mask, but his lips twitch ever so slightly. "I said no interruptions."

I cast a quick glance at Abby, my eyes lowering to the expensive rings on her wedding finger in case she needs a reminder of her marital status. "Yeah, I can see that."

"Leave." Charlie stares through me, his icy tone launching a new assault on my heart.

"Charlie!" Abby slaps his arm. "Don't be rude." She turns an intrusive lens my way as she pushes off the desk, standing behind Charlie. "Coffee wasn't necessary, but it's much appreciated. Thanks, Demi."

I give her a tight smile, and then, I spin on my heel and get the hell out of there before I do, or say, something I regret.

I flounce back to my desk, seething. I read over the transcript I've just typed, correcting the multitude of errors as I fume inside.

I'm so mad at myself for blowing that asshole and for letting him reciprocate. *Why the hell do I lose my morals and most of my brain cells the instant he touches me?* And now, he's in there with her fussing and fawning over him.

I spend an hour typing and retyping the report that I should have finished ages ago, but I can't concentrate for shit. Because Abby is *still* in there with Charlie and my mind keeps conjuring up less-than-helpful images of them together—replaying what went down between us this morning on a loop, only this time it's Abby draped across Charlie's desk and it's her pussy he's devouring.

I'm contemplating pulling a sickie and going home when Charlie's door opens, and Abby finally emerges. I pretend I don't see her, feigning absorption in something on my screen. It's rude and unprofessional, but I've got zero fucks to give right now.

The door snicks shut with a subtle click, and I tap away on my computer, listening for the telltale sounds of disappearing footfall when a form hovers over my workstation.

She clears her throat, and I look up, plastering a fake congenial smile on my face. "Can I help you, Mrs. Anderson?"

She tosses her long dark hair over one shoulder. "I was hoping we could talk." She glances around. "Is there some place private we could go?"

I want to talk to her as much as I want root canal surgery, but I'm intrigued enough to do it. "Of course. Follow me." I get up, holding my shoulders back as we walk off, side by side. We don't talk, and I hate the inquisitive stares that follow us as we make our way to the conference room.

And I get it.

It's a bit like watching the Olsen twins out for a stroll.

We reach our destination, and I check the digital calendar on the wall, to ensure the room isn't booked, before opening the door and gesturing Abby inside.

I close the door behind us and turn to face her. Neither of us sits. "What's this about?" I ask, eager to get this over and done with.

"It's not what you're thinking." She stares me directly in the eyes.

"I don't know what you mean." I cross my arms over my chest.

"What you walked in on. I was just talking to him."

I bite back my snort of hilarity, adopting Charlie's cold mask of indifference. "It's none of my business."

"Oh, but I think it is." She tilts her head to the side. "I'm not blind. I saw the way you were looking at one another. There's something between you, right?"

"He's my boss. I'm his employee. That's the extent of our relationship," I lie.

She moves back, propping her butt on the edge of the table. She seems to do that a lot. She extends her slim jean-clad legs, crossing her ankles at the feet and gripping the table with both hands. "You have the upper hand here, because you know who I am, but I don't know anything about you."

I smooth a stray hair back into my chignon, not surprised to hear that. I expect I was Charlie's dirty little secret and that no one knows what went down between us Christmas night. "I don't know what you expect me to say."

"Can we just cut the crap and talk to one another honestly. From one woman who cares about Charlie to another?"

It's on the tip of my tongue to say I don't care about him, but petty retorts are a waste of my time, and I'd rather get this—whatever this is—over and done with. I push off the door and walk to her side, mirroring her position. "Just say what it is you want to say."

She turns to face me. "Was it you? Were you the woman he slept with Christmas night?"

Shock splays across my face, and my limbs almost go out from under me. "He told you about that?"

"He didn't so much tell me as I figured it out." Her lips kick up, and her eyes alight with mischief. "You left nail marks all over him, and he had obvious sex hair when he returned to the house."

I stare at her incredulously. "Why aren't you mad? I mean, I know you weren't really married, but you were together at some point."

She shakes her head. "We were never together like that. We kissed on occasion, but only when we needed to put on a show."

"I have no idea what that means."

She sighs, tucking hair behind her ears. "The world we inhabit is a fucked-up place."

"You mean the elite?" I've read everything I could get my hands on about the organization, and while a lot of it is supposition, it seems plausible when you consider the wealthy circles these people are a part of. After what came out about Epstein, it's hard to deny that anything is possible.

We live in a sick, sick world.

"Yes. Maybe someday, I'll get to tell you my story, but essentially, Charlie and I were in an arranged marriage. He didn't know I'd already married Kai, my husband, because things were strained with Charlie for a while."

"And they're not now?"

"It's complicated, Demi. I've known Charlie practically all my life. He was my brother's closest friend growing up. He made some shitty decisions, which led to a split in our friendship, but I believe in forgiveness where forgiveness is warranted, and I'm trying to fix things, but that man is a stubborn jerk." She jabs her finger in the direction of Charlie's office.

This time, it's my turn to smile. "That's putting it mildly."

She laughs. "I noticed how brash he was with you, and that's how I know."

"Know what?"

"That he's into you."

I snort out a laugh. "That is ridiculous. He's into humiliating me and making sure I know my place."

A genuine smile slips over her mouth. "Ah, I see. You're in denial too."

"This is a strange conversation," I truthfully admit.

"Yeah," she readily agrees. "Even though our wedding wasn't real, and I was in love with Kai, it still pissed me off that Charlie slept with someone else that night. It was disrespectful and inappropriate. But I was curious about his mystery woman. And now I've met you, it makes more sense."

My brows climb to my hairline. "It does? Well, maybe, you can enlighten me because I've got no idea what's going on. And while we're being brutally honest, I kind of hated you, and I was terrified you were going to show up here and call me out for sleeping with your husband. Which I didn't know, by the way, until after the deed was done," I add.

"If you're beating yourself up over it, stop now. I have no beef with either of you over that night."

"Cheating is a deal breaker for me, and I was disgusted with myself and beyond furious with him. I know the truth now, and that should help, but the fact is, Charlie believed your marriage was real and he still had sex with me. That's hardly a great character endorsement. Or the fact he's a walking STD."

She barks out a laugh. "Charlie once told me he loves sex, but that's all he's known. A purely physical act. He's never been in a relationship. I wouldn't be too quick to dismiss him." She peers into my eyes. "Despite how he treats you, Charlie is a great guy. He lost his way for a while, but he's loyal and dependable, and he would die before he let anything happen to those he loves." She looks off into space for a minute. "He nearly died protecting me," she whispers.

"What?"

"He wasn't injured by the bomb. That was the story the elite fed the media. He jumped in front of a bullet aimed at me." She stands. "I don't know what's going on between you, and I won't interfere, but if you have feelings for him, please don't give up on him. Please give him a chance to show you who he truly is. All I want is for him to be happy, and if he could have that with you..." She trails off, her hopeful eyes searching mine for answers I can't give.

I stand. "I think you're under some misapprehension, Abby. There is nothing going on between me and Charlie."

She takes my arm, pulling me over to the window. We stand side by side in front of the glass, our reflections staring back at us. "I know you've seen it. How much we look alike."

"All that proves is Charlie is still in love with you."

She turns to face me, repeatedly shaking her head. "Charlie was never in love with me. I think he believed he was, at one point, but it was tied up with the elite crap we were dealing with and his need to keep me safe. Trust me when I say the love we share is strictly platonic, because the way he looked at you back there?" Her voice elevates a few decibels as she arches a brow. "I've *never* seen Charlie look at any woman like that."

Chapter Eight
Charlie

A week passes and nothing changes although the world continues to revolve. Since her surprise visit last week, Abby is on a one-woman mission to bring me back into the crew. She calls and texts several times a day and accosts me every time I step foot on campus, and it's clear she's not giving up until I concede something.

"Why does it matter so much to you?" I say as we stand in line in the food court at lunchtime on Monday.

"Because you're my friend, *our* friend, and I don't want you to be alone."

"Save your pity for someone who cares," I deadpan, swiping two chocolate muffins on a whim and plonking them on my tray.

"It's not pity, and you're not fooling me, Charlie." She shoots me a smug grin. "I can keep this up forever. You, of all people, know how stubborn I can be."

My lips twitch at the truth. "I doubt your husband supports your plan."

I try not to hiss the word husband, but it's still a bit of a touchy subject, because I feel like such a fool every time I reflect on the whole scenario. I was a blind idiot not to see what was right in front of my eyes.

Abby was never mine, and if I'm honest with myself, I was never hers either.

At the time, I really thought what I was feeling was love, but when she was gone from my life, I realized it couldn't have been that, because the pain I felt at her loss paled in comparison to the pain of losing my family.

And while I miss having Abby around, I don't miss her much more than I've missed her brother.

She was right all along. I confused platonic love, and wanting to keep her safe, with romantic love. I was never in love with her that way. I'm glad we cleared the air last week. That she believes and agrees with me.

Maybe, I should make more of an effort.

No man actually likes being an island, and I'm getting sick of my own company.

I glance over at their usual table, finding Kaiden's eyes fixed on mine. He's not glaring at me, but it's far from a friendly look. My eyes flit to Jackson Lauder, watching his mouth curl in a sneer as a pretty girl with long dark-blonde hair walks by. Kaiden's attention switches, and he looks away from me, mouthing something at Lauder, and they get into it. I turn around, finding Abby watching me with that invasive all-seeing look of hers.

Air whooshes out of her mouth, and she rolls her eyes. "You two need to quit this shit. Holding on to your hatred is so pointless. Get over yourself already." She prods me with one slim finger in the chest. "Drew needs you. He's every bit as stubborn as me, so he won't admit it, but he needs your friendship, and for that to happen, you need to fix shit with Kai too."

I hand my items to the girl behind the register and swipe

my card. "Look." I angle my body so I'm facing her. "I appreciate the effort you're making. I genuinely do. But you can't fix this."

"*You* can." She swipes her card, paying for her lunch, as the girl hands me my takeout bag. "Starting with coming to dinner on Sunday."

I open my mouth to decline, *again*, but she clamps her hand over my lips. "I'm not taking no for an answer. Three o'clock at our place." She grabs her tray, fighting a smirk. "Bring Demi," she adds, sauntering off with a pleased smile on her face, not even allowing me to respond either way.

I'm thinking of Demi as I climb into my Land Rover and exit the college campus, heading for the city.

Then again, when am I ever not thinking about her?

It's getting worse since we went down on each other in my office last week. I've been replaying it in my mind, over and over, jerking off repeatedly to visions of her hot mouth suctioned around my dick and the addictive taste of her arousal as I ravished her pussy. Nothing has ever tasted sweeter, and I can't evict her from my mind or the craving to return for more. Desire pools in my groin, and my cock predictably responds, thickening behind my pants.

I've tried my best to keep her at arm's length this past week, but my resolve is weakening.

I know she's noticed how I avail of every opportunity to touch her. Whether it's a fleeting alignment of our bodies as I waltz past or a deliberate brush of my fingers against hers when she's handing me something or touching her arm accidentally on purpose when I lean over her desk, invading her personal space as I hover way too close for comfort, I'm having a hard time staying away from her. Fighting a daily battle not to put my hands on her.

She hasn't brought the subject up, and we've been dancing

around one another, acting all professional when both of us know there is something definitely *not* professional building between us.

Before I know it, I'm parking in my designated spot in the private garage underneath the office building, grateful I managed to ghost-drive here without getting in to an accident.

I'm mulling over Abby's dinner invitation as I stroll along the corridor toward my office. A few of the ladies look up from their desks, smiling in my direction, and I acknowledge each one of them. Dad made it his business to know all the employees by name, and it's something I've been woefully neglectful of and something I intend to rectify in the short-term.

Demi's dark head is bent over her desk as I approach. Her long, thick, glossy hair falls in soft waves around her shoulders, and a craving to bury my face in the strands and inhale the smell of that peach shampoo she uses jumps up and bites me. I linger by her desk, my hand twitching with a craving to touch her like it's an illness, and the only cure is the feel of her skin under my fingertips. She doesn't look up, and I set the paper bag down beside her with a little trepidation. "I got you a muffin," I say, clearing my throat. "I, eh, thought you might be hungry."

I drag a hand through my hair. Christ. I'm a bag of nerves, and it's pathetic. I'm never like this with women, and it makes me uneasy.

Slowly, she lifts her head up, and panic shoots through my veins when I see her swollen red-rimmed eyes and her blotchy skin. I place my laptop bag on the ground and crouch down so I'm at eye level with her. "What's wrong? Has something happened?"

She visibly gulps while shaking her head. "It's nothing. I'm fine." Her voice is barely more than a whisper.

I'm calling bullshit on that, but I don't blame her for not wanting to confide in me. I've been a total prick to her since she came to work here. She probably thinks this is an act, instead of genuine concern. "Can I get you anything? Some water or a coffee?"

She shakes her head, casting a glance at the bag. "I don't need anything. And thanks for the muffin."

I grab my bag and straighten up. "If you change your mind, let me know. And if you need to go home early, that's fine too."

Tears well in her eyes. "I'd rather work," she says, offering me a weak smile.

"Okay." I walk into my office and close the door, not fully shutting it because I want to keep an eye on her.

The longer I watch her, the more my concern grows. While she's not full-on sobbing at her desk, every so often, she tears up, dabbing at the corners of her eyes with a tissue. On other occasions, she stares absently at nothing, clearly in a different place in her mind, and she's jumpy, solemn, and most unlike herself when anyone approaches her desk.

I stare at my screen, completely lost in thought, as I wonder what's going on. If I had to guess, it's something to do with her father although I could be completely offtrack. Something has always bothered me about her father's exit from the business, and stuff Demi has said has been nagging me a lot lately. I call Arthur. "Are you busy?"

"No more than usual," he replies.

"You got five minutes? I want to ask you something."

"My door is always open to you, Charles."

My stomach drops to my toes, and I almost tell him to forget it, but this is more urgent than my sensitivity.

I can't work out whether Arthur calls me Charles out of habit, some misguided sense of respect, or if he's fucking with me because he sees how much I hate to be reminded of my father.

Which is all kinds of wrong, because he was a great father. Not perfect, but family was everything to him, and any mistakes he made were done in the name of protecting his family. Familiar feelings of guilt, pain, and remorse threaten to smother me, and I grip the edge of my desk tightly, digging my nails in, needing something to ground me in the moment, to pull me out of my head.

"I'll be right there," I manage to spit out after a brief silence, hanging up.

I step out of my office, faltering for a second when I glance at Demi's dejected form. I want to go to her, to offer words of comfort, but I'll only sound like a broken record, and I sense she just wants to be left alone to deal with whatever it is.

I rap twice on Arthur's door before entering, inwardly groaning when I see Corrinna Smith seated in front of Arthur's desk, gathering a handful of files.

"I can come back," I say from the doorway.

Arthur gestures me inside with a nod of his head. "It's fine. We were just finished." He looks at our chief human relations officer. "Thanks, Corrinna. Keep me apprised of the situation."

"Of course. Thanks for your time."

She rises, walking toward me with a wide smile. "Mr. Barron." She casts an appreciative glance at me before brushing past, her arm purposely touching mine.

The door closes, and Arthur chuckles. "I think you have a fan."

I drop down into the chair she vacated, scoffing. "She should know it won't be reciprocated." She has subtly hit on me at a couple of company events, but I haven't entertained that idea. She's not my type, and she's an added complication I could do without. "I don't shit where I eat," I add.

"Unless it comes to Ms. Alexander." Arthur shoots me a knowing look.

"I'm sure I don't know what you mean. I'm aware of the no-fraternization policy, and I'm not one to break the rules."

Not usually. But I have hardly given company policy any thought in my quest to get down and dirty with Demi. Although, in my defense, anything that's happened between us has been impulsive and a spur-of-the-moment thing.

I wonder if he heard something last week, when we were devouring one another in my office. The door was closed, but he was the only other person on the floor at that time.

"The ladies love to gossip, and the friction between you and your assistant hasn't gone unnoticed. Some contend it's a ploy to hide the fact you're fucking her."

"It sounds like bullshit to me, and maybe, we need to give those ladies more work to occupy their time."

"Spoken like a true Barron," he quips.

"Speaking of." I sit up straighter in my chair. "Do you know any of the details behind Henry Alexander's exit from the business?"

He does a piss-poor job of hiding his smug smile. "Your father handled that with Corrinna and the legal department. What is it you want to know?"

"It seems he was quick to get rid of him, and that's not in keeping with what I know about my father. He was a man of the people. He valued hard work, integrity and loyalty, and he was good to his staff, so I find it odd that he was apparently keen to lose a good financial controller."

Arthur shrugs. "Like I said, I wasn't involved. It was most likely a cost-saving measure. Your father loved making money as much as he loved his employees. Soren Phillips is probably on half the salary Henry was on."

That may very well be true because the man is only in his

late twenties and he doesn't have the years of experience Demi's dad had under his belt. But it still doesn't sit right with me. It hasn't for some time, and I need to get to the bottom of it.

"Thanks." I stand.

"You could always ask Corrinna. I'm sure she'd be more than agreeable to sitting down, one to one, to discuss it."

I bark out a laugh. "Yeah. Thanks, but no thanks." I walk toward the door.

"Say hello to Demi for me," he calls out, and I flip him the bird over my shoulder.

His loud laughter follows me out into the corridor.

Demi isn't at her desk when I return, so I close my office door and spend a half hour reflecting on everything as an idea grows wings. I make a quick phone call, and then, I grab my keys and head out.

Demi is tapping away on her keyboard when I appear in front of her. "I have to go out."

She frowns, glancing at the clock on the wall. "What, now?"

I nod. "Yep. I'll be back later."

"But what about your four o'clock with Simon Reed?"

Damn. I'd forgotten that was today, but this is more urgent. Mr. Reed can wait. "Reschedule it."

"But—"

"No buts, Ms. Alexander. Handle it."

She narrows her eyes at me, and her lips thin, and I silently fist pump the air. I'll take her annoyance over sadness any day.

I walk into the plush, modern high-rise across town, approach the reception desk, and ask for Xavier Daniels.

Xavier is Abby's best friend and a tech nerd genius. He

graduated from Rydeville University last May top of his class, walking straight into a job with Techxet, the company owned by Sawyer Hunt's father. Sawyer Hunt is Kaiden Anderson's best friend, along with Jackson Lauder.

Techxet recently established a new branch in Boston and Xavier was one of the first employees recruited. I have no clue what exactly he does, as I was already estranged from my crew by then, but knowing how skilled he is, I'm betting it's a prestigious position.

Xavier emerges from an elevator on my left a few minutes later, walking toward me with a shit-eating grin on his mouth. He's wearing ripped, black skinny jeans, scuffed boots with the laces unopened, and a crumpled AC/DC T-shirt that looks like it hasn't seen a washing machine in a few centuries.

"Well, well," he says, halting in front of me. "If it isn't the illustrious Charlie Barron."

I stand. "I'd say you're looking good, but it's best not to start this conversation with a lie." I purposely give him a quick once-over. "They let you dress like that at work?"

He lifts his shoulder, motioning me to walk with him. "Look around," he says as we head toward the elevator he just got out of. "Everyone dresses casually. There is no dress code around here except come as you are."

"Sounds like your kind of place," I mock as we step into the elevator.

"It is." He grins, winking as he stabs the button for the top floor. He eyes my fitted charcoal-gray suit with unconcealed disdain. "If I had to dress like that every day, I'd slit my wrists."

"Wow. Tell me how you really feel."

The elevator pings, and we step out into a large, open-plan office with floor-to-ceiling windows on three sides. I whistle under my breath. "This is all yours?"

"You likey?" He guides me over to two large gamer chairs resting off to one side of the space.

"It's very you," I say, removing my jacket and rolling up the sleeves of my shirt. "It looks like a paint can exploded in here or you let your inner graffiti artist loose."

Strips of vibrant colors decorate the walls in a haphazard fashion. Like someone stood in front of the wall and threw pots of paint at it. The floors are natural hardwood floors, unstained and marked with scratches and dents giving it a lived-in feel even though this building is a relatively new build. All the furniture is eclectic and unmatching. But it works.

"I think that's a compliment," Xavier drawls, popping a can of soda and handing it to me.

"It is. I like it. It's got personality."

Xavier positively beams as he opens another soda. "I designed it myself. Abby helped." He chuckles to himself. "Hunt almost had a coronary when he saw it. It offends his delicate sensibilities."

I smirk, remembering the dynamic between those two. "You tapping that yet?"

Xavier grins. "A gentleman never tells."

"I'll take that as a yes."

He waggles his brows, slurping noisily from his soda. "Enjoyable as this is, I doubt you came here to discuss my flamboyant sex life."

"I need a favor, and I was hoping you still took on private paid jobs."

"When I have time," he adds, losing the smirk and pinning me with an earnest look. "And I've got to say, I'm surprised you sought me out."

"You're the best, and I trust you to keep this confidential," I say, removing the envelope from my inside jacket pocket. It's why I didn't ask anyone in the IT department at the bank to investigate. I don't want anyone in the company knowing I'm digging into this.

"I haven't agreed to shit," he supplies, crossing one leg over the other.

"You'll be handsomely rewarded for your time."

"Money has never been my greatest motivator."

I level him with a dry look. "What will it take for you to do this?"

"Say please." I stare at him, and he laughs, smoothing his fingers along the taut peaks of his faux hawk. It's green today, but Xavier changes his hair color as often as the weather. "I'm serious."

"Still fucking weird," I mumble, sighing. I claw my hands through my hair. "Fine. *Please* can you investigate this for me."

He reaches out, snatching the envelope from me. "That wasn't so hard."

I flip him the bird while he's hunched over.

"Talk me through it."

"Henry Alexander is an ex-employee of my father's. He was exited in a hurry just after he'd had a stroke. It wasn't like my father to treat a loyal employee so callously. I'd like to know if there is more to it."

He lifts his head. "Why do you care?"

I wet my dry lips. "His daughter works for me, and I sense something has happened. I'd like to understand what's going on, to know if I need to revisit his case. If we should've done more."

He places the documents on his lap, leans back, and stares at me. "I'll do it—on one condition." I wait for him to continue. "You come to dinner on Sunday. It would mean the world to Abby."

"You two gossip like a couple of old women," I grumble.

He shrugs. "We tell each other everything, and she'd be delighted you came to me today."

"You can't tell her or anyone."

He begins rummaging through the paperwork again. "I never divulge details of the stuff I'm working on. My reputation rests on my discretion."

My shoulders relax. "Fine. I'll come to dinner."

His eyes pop wide as he pulls out the photo of Demi. I slide my suddenly sweaty palms over my thighs, waiting for his reaction.

"Shit." He brings the picture closer, examining it in more detail. "Abby wasn't kidding. They are so incredibly alike."

"It's not what you're thinking."

He lifts his gaze to me. "Hey, I'm a judgment-free zone." His lips kick up. "But Anderson is going to flip his shit when he sees her. Hope you've got big balls, Charlie boy, because you're going to need them."

Chapter Nine
Demi

"Thank you so much for your time, Mr. Reed, and apologies again that Mr. Barron couldn't be here." I shake the man's hand as we wait for the elevator to arrive.

"Emergencies happen, and if he hadn't been called away, I wouldn't have had the pleasure of your lovely company."

The elevator pings, and the door opens. "I'll be sure to update Mr. Barron, and I'll be in touch."

He nods affably. "I look forward to hearing from you. Please reiterate my eagerness to work with Barron Banking and Financial Investment Services."

"I will pass the message on."

I wait until the doors have closed before returning to my desk.

"What the hell are you thinking?" Margaret Ann whispers as she leans over my desk.

I glance around quickly, but no one is in earshot. "I know Mr. Fleming is keen to review Simon Reed's proposal. Charlie had an emergency," I lie. "So, I covered for him. It's no biggie."

"You could get fired for this!" She shakes her head. "It's not your place to conduct meetings in place of the president."

"I'll only get fired if someone rats me out." I drill her with a pointed look.

"You know I won't say anything, but anyone could've spotted you with him in the conference room."

"I'll take my chances."

Truth is, the man showed up an hour early for the meeting, narrowly missing Charlie, and I didn't have it in my heart to turn him away.

To be honest, I was also grateful for the distraction. I've been a basket case since the appointment this morning.

Dad's physician isn't very optimistic about his chances of survival. Without the experimental drug, he said Dad has three to six months left to live.

Pain stabs me in the heart as I recall his words and his confirmation that we need two hundred K to participate in the drug trial. Our fundraising plans seem pitiful now. There is no way I can raise that kind of money in time. I've been wracking my brain all day to come up with a solution, but short of robbing a bank—pun intended—we're all out of options.

I somehow managed to hold my tears at bay this morning, but as soon as I'd dropped Dad off at home, I drove to the office and broke down in my car in the parking lot.

I know I looked a mess when I rocked up to work, and maybe, I should've taken Charlie up on his offer to go home, but I can't face Dad. Can't face what I know he's going to say. He will put me first, like he always does, and I can't let him console me when he's the one who is dying.

Subconsciously, I think I took that meeting, in part, because it will delay the inevitable. Danny is visiting Dad tonight, so I can stay late and type up a post-meeting report. Charlie will probably freak when he finds out what I've done. Until he calms down and realizes I've done him a favor.

"Be careful, Demi," she murmurs. "I know how much you need this job, and people are already gossiping about you and the boss man."

"They are? Why?" That's news to me.

"He's different with you."

"He hates me."

"There's a fine line between love and hate." Her eyes twinkle with mirth. "Besides, someone who hates you doesn't notice, and indulge, your weakness for chocolate muffins." She squeezes my shoulder before walking back to her workstation.

Charlie handing me that did surprise me even if I didn't show it because I was numb at the time. But it was a thoughtful gesture.

I dig into the muffin as I review my notes from the meeting, along with the materials Simon Reed brought with him. He's also emailed me his presentation, and I print a copy to give to Charlie tomorrow along with my report and recommendations.

I'm immersed in my work, putting my finishing touches to the file I've prepared, long after everyone has left the office, so I don't notice Charlie returning. It's well after seven, and I presumed he'd called it a night. He always leaves early on a Monday to attend to some regular appointment.

"Demi. What are you still doing here?" he asks, stopping by my desk. He's lost his jacket and tie, and the sleeves of his pristine white dress shirt are rolled up to his elbows, showcasing his tan, muscular arms.

"I stayed late to finish a report," I say, scurrying to put the printed material into the folder before he sees. But it's too late, because his gaze lands on the presentation, and his brow instantly puckers.

"What is this?" he demands.

I bite on the inside of my cheek as pressure settles on my chest. "Mr. Reed arrived early, a couple of minutes after you left, actually. It felt rude to turn him away. And I'm aware of how eager the board is to hear the details of his proposal." Charlie knows I type up the minutes from the board meetings. My throat is parched, and I wet my dry lips. "So, I met with him, took notes, and asked questions, and I've just typed up a proposal. I was planning on giving it to you tomorrow."

He stares at me, wearing that nonchalant mask, and as the seconds tick by, my heart rate accelerates, blood pounds in my ears, and I'm scarcely breathing.

He's going to fire me for insubordination. For overstepping the mark.

After what feels like eternity, he finally speaks. "Do you need to leave? Or could you talk me through it now?"

"You're not mad?" I stupidly blurt.

His lips thin. "I didn't say that. I'll reserve judgment for now."

"I just need to print this last document. I'll follow you in."

He bobs his head before entering his office. I print the report with shaking hands, urging myself to calm down. I need to keep a cool head to talk him through this and pray he doesn't can my cheeky ass.

I double-check I have everything I need before stepping into the lion's den.

Charlie is quiet and attentive as I talk him through it, outlining the benefits of the system and how I believe it will cut regulatory processing times in half, thereby adding to the bottom line. I provide the quick cost assessment I've prepared along with a list of references Simon emailed to me after the meeting. While his current clients are smaller in size and scope, it seems he has the capacity to scale, provided we assign the appropriate IT and business management resources to work on the implementation.

Silence filters through the air when I finish. Charlie drums his fingers on the desk, looking pensive as he stares at me. I wait with bated breath for him to say something. When he does speak, I'm completely caught off guard.

"Have you eaten?"

I blink repeatedly as I stare at him. He arches a brow when I don't reply. "Ah, does the muffin count?"

He stands, swiping his keys. "No. I'm taking you to dinner."

My brows knit together and I stay rooted in my seat. "What about my report?"

He extends his hand. "We can discuss it while we eat. I'm starving."

I take his hand in a bit of a daze, letting him haul me to my feet. He watches as I switch off my computer, grab my coat and purse, and follow him to the elevator. I stare straight ahead as the elevator lowers, wondering what the heck is going on.

When we reach the parking garage, I turn left, in the direction of my car. "I'll drive," Charlie says. "You can leave your car here overnight, and I'll send someone to pick you up in the morning."

"I'd rather follow you," I say. "I can't stay out too late. I need to get home to my father. And I need my car in case of an emergency."

His features soften a little. "Of course. No problem."

I trail him out of the parking garage, all the way back to Rydeville, surprised when he pulls in to a small Italian restaurant on the outskirts of town. It's a little off the beaten path, but I know the place. Dad took me here for my nineteenth birthday, a few weeks after the place opened. The décor isn't much to write home about, but the food is authentic and delicious.

I park my beloved old Volvo behind Charlie's expensive

brand-new Land Rover, tapping out a quick text to Danny before I get out.

Charlie takes my hand as if it's the most natural thing in the world, and we walk hand in hand to the door without speaking.

"Mr. Barron." The owner, a small man with a mop of thick gray hair, greets us at the door. "We have your table ready."

I pin Charlie with a curious look. "I called on the way," he explains.

The restaurant is half empty, but I guess that's normal for a Monday night.

We are seated at a small circular booth at the back. The owner takes my coat and Charlie's jacket before handing us menus and leaving a chilled bottle of water on the table.

I skim my eyes over the menu. "The spaghetti with sausage is good," Charlie says.

"Dad enjoyed that the last time we were here."

"I didn't think many people know about this place," he supplies, pouring me a glass of water. "It's a shame, because the food is so good."

"It is, but the location sucks."

He grins. "Your instincts and observations are always on point, Demi."

Wow. That sounds remarkably like a compliment, but I'm not used to those from him, so I wonder if it's a veiled insult. "No need to sound so surprised," I say, sipping my water. "I do have a working brain. I was in the top ten percent in most of my classes in college."

"I didn't mean to insult you." He leans forward on his elbows. "I have wondered why you took on a personal assistant position when it's outside your field of study."

"I didn't have much of a choice, and it was the only open position available in the company that I could conceivably do," I explain, as a waiter arrives to take our order. I go for the spinach and mushroom ravioli, and Charlie orders the spaghetti and sausage dish.

"Because of your father?"

I nod. "Dad was my only parent, and he always put me first. Now, it's my turn."

"What about your mother?" he quietly asks.

"She died from complications arising from my birth."

"I'm sorry."

"Don't be. I had a great childhood. Dad was an amazing father, and he did his best to make sure I wanted for nothing, especially his love."

"That sounds a lot like my parents, which is unusual if you understood the world I grew up in."

I'm no fan of Charlie's dad, for obvious reasons, but that doesn't mean I can't be compassionate. "You must miss him. I heard you were close."

A slash of pain crosses his handsome face. "I do," he says in a quiet voice. "Family is everything."

"It is." I grin, nudging his shoulder, wanting to defuse the sudden tense atmosphere and needing to wipe that sad look off his face. "Look at us getting along. You're actually talking to me instead of biting my head off."

"Careful, Bumbling. The night is young."

I laugh. "You know, we don't have to be enemies."

He takes a drink of his water before turning his gorgeous green eyes on me. "I don't want to be, but sometimes, it's the easiest route."

"Why?"

"Because indulging my feelings isn't something I'm good at. The last time I tried, it majorly backfired."

"You mean Abby?" I risk asking, and he nods. Silence descends, and I sip my water.

"That guy from the club," he says. "Is he your boyfriend?"

"It's a little late to be asking me that, don't you think?"

He smiles, a proper, relaxed smile, and I melt at how his entire face comes alive. He slides his arm along the back of the booth behind me. "Perhaps."

"He's my ex," I explain. "I don't cheat."

The smile drops off his face, and he removes his arm, a muscle clenching in his jaw.

Still, I'm not sorry I said it.

It's the truth, and there's no beating around the bush. Charlie cheated on Abby, and whatever this attraction is between us can't lead anywhere. Because I don't date cheaters or guys who treat me like shit, especially after intimacy. And there's the matter of him being my boss and his father being the one who kicked my dad when he was already down.

"I know you must think the worst of me," he says, turning to face me. "And no excuse will explain it away, but my father had just died, and I was devastated. I had no one to turn to. And then you were there, offering me comfort when I needed it. I made some bad decisions, which contributed to my father's death." He hangs his head, and tension bleeds into the air.

I don't understand what he means, because I thought Mr. Barron died of a heart attack.

"The pain and guilt were crushing me," he continues, rubbing at this chest as he gives me his attention again. "I desperately needed an escape. It was selfish and wrong, but I don't regret it because you gave me hope that night at a time when I'd lost all faith in humanity."

"Didn't you regret it at all?" I ask, because honestly, if he could do that and not feel any remorse, he is not someone I want to get involved with.

"By the bucketload at first," he says, helping to ease my discomfort. "I was unfair to you and Abby. I'm not proud of my actions, and for a while, I thought it was the reason why she was holding back." His eyes burn with indecipherable emotion. Tentatively, he takes my hand, lacing our fingers together. Warmth seeps into my skin, embedding bone deep. "I blamed you, which was so wrong, but it was easier than facing up to my own culpability."

"That's why you were so mean to me."

He bobs his head. "And then, it was just easier to continue lashing out instead of confronting my feelings." He rubs his thumb back and forth across the top of my hand, but I'm not even sure he realizes he's doing it.

"What are you saying?"

He shrugs, smiling nervously. "I don't really know. You should run a million miles from me, Demi. I'm fucked up in the head."

"You're really selling it to me here," I joke.

The waiter brings our plates then, and it's the perfect moment to break up the conversation.

I miss the warmth of his touch as we separate our fingers. We eat in silence, but it's not awkward like it was at the start. We're both deep in thought. I'm beginning to see there is a lot more to Charlie than the exterior he presents.

"I know it's probably too late," he says, out of the blue, "but I'm sorry."

"For what exactly?" I ask, spearing another ravioli.

"For everything cruel I've said and done, and I promise things will be different from now on."

"Why the change of heart? And why now?"

He shrugs, chewing slowly on his pasta. After he's swallowed, he sets his fork down and scrubs a hand over his jaw. "I've been fighting everyone, pushing them all away, believing it's better like that, and punishing myself because I believed I deserved it." His chest heaves as he pauses for a couple beats. His eyes dive into mine, and he's hiding nothing from me now.

"I'm tired of fighting," he admits, tucking my hair behind my ear. "I don't want to fight with you anymore."

"What *do* you want?" My voice comes out all breathy.

He brushes his thumb across my cheek. "I want to feel something real. To stop feeling like I'm the one who died."

"Oh, Charlie." I cup his face, and my heart aches for him. The sheer vulnerability on his face tells me he's being one hundred percent honest right now, and I'd challenge anyone to remain cold-hearted when confronted with this truth.

Charlie is lonely. He has no one in his corner, and he desperately needs that to start believing in himself.

He presses his forehead to mine, and I close my eyes, breathing him in.

"I don't know how to do this, Demi, and I can't offer you much, but all I know is I need you in my life."

I open my eyes, cupping his face. "Maybe, we need each other," I say, thinking of the tough road ahead. "And we can figure it out as we go along."

Chapter Ten
Charlie

I arrive at the office, after college, the following lunchtime, feeling more nervous than the time I lost my virginity, at thirteen, to an older woman, in a room full of pervert elite looking to get their rocks off by proxy.

"Ms. Alexander," I say, pausing briefly at Demi's desk.

She looks up and smiles. "Mr. Barron."

"Could I see you in my office, please. Bring the regulatory report with you."

"Of course."

I stalk into my office, blatantly ignoring the hushed whispers and finger-pointing, because nothing is taking away my good mood. I slept better last night than I have in the past six months.

Unburdening some of the shit in my head to Demi felt good.

Being in her company felt good.

Not kissing her goodnight didn't.

And not prying into whatever upset her yesterday didn't

feel good either. I tried getting her to open up, but she clammed up tight, and I didn't push.

I know I have a lot to do to earn her trust, and this peace is new between us, but I'm determined to win her over.

She steps into my office like a ray of sunlight. I almost gag at my thought, and I cough to disguise the burst of laughter that escapes my mouth. She eyes me like I'm cray-cray, and I don't blame her. She must think I'm a freaking schizo.

"Hey." She smiles, and it takes colossal willpower not to cross the room and grab her in my arms. I want to kiss her so badly. Do all kinds of naughty shit to her. But I rein my hormones in. Pouncing on her got me into a world of trouble the first time. I'm determined to do right by her now.

"Hey. How are you feeling today?"

"I'm good," she says, smiling, but I still see pain hiding behind her eyes.

"I know this ceasefire is new between us, but you can talk to me about anything."

She sits down in front of my desk, placing the file on the empty chair beside her. "About that. Some of the girls are talking."

"I heard." I tap my fingers off my chin as I lean back in my chair. "Let them gossip."

"See, I have an issue with that."

"Go on."

"Some of them already feel like I only have this job because of who my dad is. The last thing I want is people thinking I'm only holding on to it because I'm banging the boss."

I lean forward, hitting her with my most seductive look. The one that usually renders woman into a pile of goo. But, so far, Demi has surprised me with her unpredictability, so who knows what reaction I'll get from her. "Speaking as your boss, I have zero issue with that."

She swats my arm. "That kind of talk will get us both into trouble. And quit with the sleazy look. It's creepy."

I burst out laughing. She is so refreshing. So down to earth. So sweet. Way too good for me. But I'm a selfish prick, so I disregard all negative thoughts. "Just to be clear, are you opposed to the act altogether or just opposed to the notion of others thinking that?"

"Now, you're propositioning me?" She folds her arms and glares at me.

Shit. I'm already failing at this. "Fuck. I'm fucking this up already. I told you I wasn't good at this and... Why are you grinning?"

"Because this new you is far too easy to wind up. Man, this is gonna be so much fun."

I purse my lips and drill her with a sharp look. "I'm still the same man. Continue talking like that and I'll take you over my knee and spank you." A red flush creeps over her cheeks, and she squeezes her thighs together. "Ah, I see." I lean even closer. "I'll add spanking to the list."

"List?" she croaks.

I stand and round the desk, perching my butt on the edge, and I lean down, right into her face. "The list of things I'm going to do to you."

She squirms in her seat, and her cheeks inflame. "You can't say stuff like that to me in the workplace!"

I get all up in her face, and my eyes drift to her succulent mouth. "But it's okay outside the office?"

"I, ah." She shoves at my chest, pushing me back, looking completely flustered. "We need another list. Rules for professional conduct in the workplace!"

I smirk, crossing my feet at the ankles, as I run the tip of one finger up her arm. "We already have one of those. I'll request a copy for you from the HR department."

"I already have a copy of it, along with the no-fraternization policy."

"Pfft." I wave my hand in the air. "I'll get rid of it."

Her mouth drops open. "You can't get rid of a company policy because you want to sleep with one of the employees!" she splutters. "You wouldn't!"

"I can and I would." I remove my finger from her tempting flesh and sit back in my chair, adjusting the semi in my pants before she notices. "But you're right. We should make some rules. I don't want this impacting you negatively. When you're promoted, I want people to know it's because you are skilled and you've earned it. Not because you're banging the boss." I flash her my pearly whites, and a surge of warmth spreads across my chest. The workplace is already infinitely more enjoyable now we've stopped being mortal enemies.

"Promotion? What promotion?" she squeaks.

"None yet, but it's only a matter of time. Your work ethic and sharp mind haven't gone unnoticed, and that report you presented yesterday was excellent." We never did get around to discussing it last night, because we were too busy getting to properly know one another. She glows from my praise, and it feels good to put a smile on her face.

Goddamn it. I'm turning into a pussy already.

"I'm not in trouble?" she asks.

"In the future, run it by me first. On this occasion, if anyone asks, you had my permission to conduct that meeting in my absence." I hold out my hand. "Hand me the file. There are a few tweaks I'd like you to make, and once I've approved the final version, you can distribute it to the board. I'd also like you to set a follow-up meeting with Simon Reed for sometime later this week. I need to meet with him myself before I sit down with the board to recommend your proposal."

She radiates enthusiasm as we run through a few sections,

verbally agreeing to changes, and her obvious delight in the work is a major turn-on, as is her intelligence.

She's at the door, ready to leave, when I pluck up the courage to say what I want to say. "Don't make plans for Sunday afternoon."

She turns around, eyeing me suspiciously. "Why?"

"Because Abby has invited us to dinner, and I'd really like you to be there."

She freezes on the spot, and I get up, walking to her. "I won't force you if you really don't want to go, but I'm not sure I can face it without you." I'm cutting myself open and bleeding at her feet again.

"But they're your friends. I don't know them, and what are they going to think when they see me?"

I cup the back of her head. "That I'm a lucky bastard."

"Charlie." She uses her no-nonsense voice on me.

I press my lips to hers in a quick kiss, not wanting to break the rules already but needing to reassure her the best way I know how. "It will be okay, I promise. And if you're uncomfortable, we can leave." She's not convinced. I can see it in her eyes. "Abby already knows about us, and if you are worried about her, you—"

"I'm not worried about her," she interjects. "We've spoken, and I like her."

My eyes almost bug out of my head. "When she was here or some other time?"

"When she was here. We cleared the air but..." She looks away.

I tilt her chin up. "But what?"

She scrunches up her nose. "I need you to be honest with me. What is happening between us, and is it because I look like her? Is she the one you want? Because I won't be second best for anyone."

"Come sit back down." I take her hand and pull her over to the couch, sitting down beside her. I grip both her hands in mine, drawing a deep breath, as I prepare to pry my chest open and expose my heart. "I have feelings for you, Demi, and I love spending time with you. I want to get to know you better. I want to take you out on dates and show you that the version of me you've seen so far is not the man I am. I can't promise you what'll happen because I have no experience with dating, but I want to try with you, and that's a first for me."

"Do you really mean that?"

"Yes. I do." I gently squeeze her hands.

"Is it because I look like her? Are you still hung up on Abby?"

"I've always been drawn to pretty brunettes with dark eyes. You're most definitely my type. And, yes, I'll admit I was first attracted to you because you reminded me of Abby. But that's not who I see when I look at you now."

I extract my hands from hers, sliding them up the side of her neck, clasping her face in my large palms. "I see *you*, Demi. You are incredibly beautiful and, hands down, the most stunning woman I've ever known. You take my breath away." A light blush stains her cheeks as she basks in my compliment. "But it's much more than your looks. I see a smart girl who selflessly quit college to look after her father. I see a girl struggling to manage all the demands placed on her, but she never complains, and she never wallows in self-pity. You have amazing inner strength, and that calls to me on a deep level."

Her eyes turn glassy, and I'm struggling to speak over the lump in my throat. "You turn up to work every day with a positive attitude and a big smile on your face even though your boss is a grumpy, sullen prick"—that earns me a radiant smile, and I'm almost blinded by the goodness she exudes from every pore —"and you work your butt off for this company even if this job isn't the job you had aspired to. You are committed, loyal, and hardworking, and that is one of the biggest turn-ons for a guy like me."

Her chest visibly inflates, and she clutches on to my arms.

"You're so beautiful, inside and out, and your touch does indescribable things to me." I press my forehead to hers, inhaling the delicate floral scent that is all her. "You have invaded my thoughts, and I've spent months fighting against something I now realize I stood no chance of winning." I ease back, peering into her face, as my fingers spread out, weaving through her hair. "I only fought you so hard because I wanted you so much and I couldn't even admit that to myself."

"How can you be sure now?"

"Because I can't imagine living a day without you in it. Even when I was being a jerk, the highlight of my day was coming into the office because you were here." My lips kick up. "Sparring with you made me hot as hell especially when you gave it back."

She shakes her head and rolls her eyes, but she's smiling. Her fingers touch my lips, and her expression turns solemn. "What about Abby now?"

I remove my hands from her hair, threading her fingers through mine, as I pin her with a serious look. I need her to understand this so there is no confusion going forward. "I thought, at one time, that I was in love with Abby, but I was confused, because I see now that wasn't the truth. I wanted to keep her safe, and it was never anything more than me loving her as a friend. She had a tough upbringing. Her father was a monster who made her life unbearable at times. I got an opportunity to do something about that, and then, everything got fucked up."

I wet my dry lips, not wanting to admit this, but I might as well lay it all out on the table. "My father trusted the wrong people, and it ultimately got him killed. But I interfered, thinking I was keeping Abby, my mom, and my sister, Lil, safe. All it did was accelerate the timeline. I watched my father murdered in cold blood, knowing I had a hand in it, and it's killed me every day since."

"Oh my God," she gasps, her eyes flooding with concern as shock splays across her face. "I had no idea. I'm so sorry, Charlie."

"A lot of messed-up shit happens in elite circles." Which is something I'll have to explain in more detail should things get serious between us, but there's no way I'm hitting her with that right now too. "And most of it is hidden, hence why everyone believes my father died of a heart attack, because that's what the elite wanted them to believe."

"It's not your fault." She tries to reassure me, gripping my hands tight. "You didn't pull the trigger."

I might as well have. I think it, but I don't say it out loud. I'm trying to convince her to give me, *us*, a go, and divulging my dark thoughts won't help my cause. "All this was going on around the same time I was with Abby except I was never with her like that. We never had sex."

"I know. She told me that. She also told me you got shot protecting her."

Not that I need reminding, but this is exactly why Abby has always been one of my best friends. I've been an arrogant asshole, but she's gone out of her way to mend bridges, smoothing things over with Demi without me even knowing. Whatever tension existed between us is completely gone, and I owe it to her to make more of an effort. To patch things up with her husband and her brother. To stop being so stubborn.

"Abby will always be one of my best friends, and I want to repair my friendship with her. Would you be okay with that?"

She nods. "I think so. I mean, I'd like to try. I know she's married, but I'd be lying if I said there wasn't some doubt about your feelings for her."

That's fair, and I think if the tables were reversed, I wouldn't be so charitable in her shoes.

I press my lips to hers softly. "I hate that my actions have caused you to doubt my feelings for you. All I ask is a chance to prove I'm genuine and it's real. Because I know I'm not in love with Abby. That I never was."

She still looks skeptical.

I need to do better.

I kiss her again, more passionately this time. When we break apart, I love how flushed her face is, how bright and expectant her eyes are, and how happy she looks. "I might have been confused before over how I was feeling," I say, preparing to lay it all out on the line. "But I'm not confused anymore."

I rub my thumb over her swollen lips. "Because I never felt for Abby the way I feel for you." I peer directly into her eyes. "I have never felt this deeply about any woman before, Demi. I have never wanted any woman as badly as I do you. And I have never wanted to open myself up to the possibility of something permanent in the way I want to do with you."

Chapter Eleven
Demi

"So, where's lover boy?" Xena asks me Thursday night at the fundraiser. The first step of our fundraising plan was a trivia night at the bar Bo works at. He managed to square things with his boss and get it set up in record time with help from Xena and Leo. I'm so appreciative of their support, and I didn't have the heart to tell them our plan is futile because there's no way we can raise the amount needed in time. The money will come in handy for other medical expenses anyway, and I'd be a fool to turn it down after it was already arranged.

"I didn't invite him," I admit, sipping on a beer as I wait for the trivia host to start proceedings.

"Why not?"

"I haven't told him about Dad's cancer yet."

"Why the hell not?" she adds, wiggling her fingers at Bo. He's manning the bar tonight, and he's gonna be busy because there's a full crowd.

"I was going to, but it's not like we're officially dating or anything."

"Girl, after what he said the other night, how can you even doubt that?"

I shrug, taking another mouthful of beer. I told Xena everything Charlie said to me, and quite frankly, I'm still having trouble believing it. "I want to believe it, and I want to trust in him, but I'm scared. Scared I'm going to fall for him and he's going to destroy me. My heart can't take any more hits."

"Any time you decide to let a guy in, you risk annihilation, but that's all part of falling in love." She slings her arm around my shoulders. "Every guy is a risk. You just need to decide if he's special enough to gamble your heart on."

"He is, but that doesn't eliminate my fear."

"You're going through all this shit on your own, Demi, and you need a little fun. Your dad would approve. You know he would. He worries about you so much, and he hates that he's a burden and keeping you from having a normal life. He would be pleased you're dating, and you said he already knows and approves of Charlie."

A throat clearing ends our conversation. I whip my head up, my jaw instantly slackening.

"That's great to hear," Charlie says, grinning. "So, when are you taking me home?" He waggles his brows, and his green eyes glint mischievously.

"What are you doing here?" I splutter.

"I'd think that's obvious." He pierces me with a dark look. "The more obvious question is why I had to learn about tonight from Margaret Ann. Why didn't you say anything?" He folds his arms across his lean abs. He's wearing the same clothes he had on today. A fitted blue suit with a crisp white shirt that clings to every chiseled muscle of his torso. He's lost the tie, and the top few buttons of his shirt are open, showcasing tan skin I've been up close and personal with.

"Sit your gorgeous ass down," Xena tells him, scooting farther into the booth and dragging me back with her. "You can interrogate her much more comfortably while sitting." She grins conspiratorially at Charlie. "I'm Xena by the way. Demi's bestie. We go way back."

"Nice to meet you," Charlie says, sliding into the booth beside me. "I'd introduce myself, but it appears you already know everything there is to know." A smug grin dances over his mouth.

"How do you know it's not because your reputation precedes you?" I say, needing to rib him because old habits die hard.

His shit-eating grin remains intact as he removes his jacket, folding it neatly and placing it behind him. My eyes are out on stilts as he rolls his shirt sleeves up to the elbows, and I swear he's doing it on purpose. Like he's gotten into my head and he knows how much his arms turn me on.

I know most women are into a broad chest, a six-pack, and those little V indents some guys have. I admire those traits too, and Charlie has all that, but his arms and hands do funny things to my insides. Maybe, it's because his arms are muscular, tanned, and strong with the perfect amount of dark hair. Or it's his manly hands, long slim fingers, and neat fingernails that get my juices going. Or it's how skillful those hands are and how they make me feel trailing all over my body.

Whatever it is, Charlie's arms are my porn, and somehow, the sneaky bastard has discovered my secret. At least now, I understand why he's always rolling his shirt up to his elbows.

"You're drooling, babe," Xena says, making zero effort to keep her voice low so he doesn't hear. "Not that I'm denying there is cause to drool, but you look like a dog in heat, and that shit's never attractive."

Charlie throws back his head, laughing. Xena grins, ignoring my pout and the punch I land on her upper arm. "What's your poison, Charlie," she asks, rising. "My man is behind the bar, so I'll get an order in."

Charlie orders a beer, handing her a fifty-dollar bill, telling her to get a drink for me and her too. As soon as she is gone, I quickly fill him in on her ménage situation because Leo is due to arrive anytime.

"Good for her," Charlie says, winking. "As long as you don't go getting ideas, Bumbling." He leans in close to my face, and I stop breathing. "Because I won't share you. Not ever."

"Duly noted." I can't contain my grin, and I'm not unhappy he came.

He takes my hand under the table. "Why didn't you mention this to me? It seems like something you should tell the guy you're dating."

"*Are* we dating?"

He wraps his arm around my waist, drawing me in close. "Were you not listening the other night? I thought I made myself clear, but if I didn't, yes, we're dating." His gaze cuts through me. "Exclusively."

"Also duly noted."

He raises our conjoined hands to his lips. "Good. Anything else we need to clear up?" His eyes glint with amusement.

"Nothing I can think of, and I'm not in the habit of keeping anything from my boyfriend, because keeping stuff secret is a recipe for disaster."

"Amen to that," he agrees before planting his lips on mine and kissing me in a way that is definitely not socially acceptable.

"Whoa. Get a room," Xena jokes, forcing us apart. She places our drinks down, fanning herself. "I think my ovaries just overheated."

"I arrived at the perfect time then," Leo says, coming up behind her and sliding his arms around her waist.

The trivia host kicks off proceedings, and we form a team with Leo and Xena. The night flows by fast, and although we don't win—much to Charlie's disgust because we were only one point behind the team who did win—I'm having the best night. The drinks are flowing, conversation is lively, and Charlie is incredibly attentive. He insists on paying for all my drinks and never lets me go near the bar, and he even insists on following me out to the ladies' room, standing guard outside.

The night draws to a close far too quickly for my liking, but the event was a roaring success, and we raised over ten thousand dollars. I have a sneaking suspicion Charlie made a large donation, but I don't ask because donations are private and it'd be rude to question him and seem ungrateful.

"I like him," Xena says when he goes to the bathroom. "I didn't expect to. Not after the way he's treated you, but I do. However, all bets are off if he hurts you."

"He seems like a good guy," Leo adds. "And let's not think the worst." He pins her with a cautionary look.

"He's sooo into you," Xena adds. "I think someone's gonna get lucky tonight," she singsongs.

I snort. "Not very likely. I've got to get home to relieve Mrs. Griffin, and I'm already going to be late."

"I can drop you home," Charlie says, coming up behind me. "I have a driver outside."

"Oooh. He has a driver outside," Xena teases.

"I can give you guys a ride home too," he offers.

"Thanks, handsome." She smushes his cheeks in her hands. "But we're gonna hang around and wait for Bo to finish his shift." She leans in to his ear, pretending to be quiet. "Leaving you free to ravish my beautiful, sexy, in-desperate-need-of-a-pounding friend on the ride home."

"I can hear you," I drawl. "And you're dead to me."

"You're supposed to, and no, I'm not." She yanks me into a fierce hug. "You need to climb that hottie like he's Mount Everest."

I roll my eyes, pointing at Leo. "No more beer for her."

Leo chuckles, slapping Charlie on the back. "Good to meet you, man. You should drop by our place with Demi sometime."

I grab Charlie out of there after we make vague promises to hang out with them some other time.

Charlie circles his arms around me, guiding me across the road to his chauffeur-driven Merc.

"I like your friends," he says once we are securely stowed in the back seat and Charlie has given my address to the driver.

"They're great, and they've been really supportive the past few months."

His arm goes around me again, and I rest my head on his shoulder. "I wish you'd told me about your dad. I didn't even know he had cancer. That's why you were upset on Monday?"

I nod as lancing pain rips across my chest. "I took him to the hospital for his appointment that morning. The doctor said he only has three to six months to live. The cancer has ravaged his body."

"I'm so fucking sorry, Demi. Can I help?"

I almost blurt the words out. About how much money we need, but I can't do it, because he might feel obligated to help, and as much as I love my dad, I'm not prostituting myself to get him the medicine he needs. And I don't want Charlie thinking I'm dating him because he's rich and he can dig us out of a hole.

What kind of start to a relationship would that be?

Plus, I don't want Charlie feeling guilty. We both know if his dad hadn't fired mine that the situation might be very different. But that's not on Charlie, and he's already carrying enough guilt where his dad is concerned.

"Just hold me," I say. "Just be there for me."

"That I can do, babe." He buries his nose in my hair as he snakes his arms firmly around my body.

We stay locked in our embrace, and I can't remember the last time I felt so content with a guy. It's surreal to think we spent months fighting the connection between us.

"You're not going to ravish me?" I half-joke as we enter the outskirts of Rydeville a short while later.

He cups my face, forcing my eyes to his. "Believe me, I want to, but I'm determined to do this right. We should have dated first before we had sex, and I want to wipe the slate clean. To start over and do it properly this time."

"How do you do that? Go from being the devil to Prince Charming?" I kiss the corner of his mouth.

"I've never wanted to be anyone's Prince Charming before, but I want to be yours," he says over my mouth before his lips descend on mine. And I lose all sense of time and reason as he kisses me passionately, pouring everything he's feeling in to every sweep of his lips, every brush of his tongue, every taste, and every moan.

And I'm in heaven. No one has ever kissed me like this or made my toes curl and my body purr so potently with the barest of touches.

Charlie's lips glide smoothly against mine, and I could stay here forever, only coming up for air when it's a necessity.

When we eventually break apart, a couple of miles from my house, we stare intently at one another, clinging to each other, and he's shielding nothing from me now. His once life-less face is awash with emotion, and it's almost too much. He sits back, bringing me with him, wrapping his protective arms around me again, pressing kisses into my hair and sighing contentedly.

I close my eyes, siphoning his warmth and his strength,

soaring on cloud nine, basking in our developing connection, praying and hoping this is the real deal and that it isn't too good to be true.

Chapter Twelve
Charlie

"There is a Xavier Daniels here to see you although he doesn't have an appointment," Demi says when I pick up the desktop phone.

"It's fine. You can send him in. Ensure I'm not disturbed."

Demi ushers Xavier into the office with a bright smile, closing the door behind us.

"She's hot." Xavier ambles toward my desk with a knowing grin on his face and a battered laptop bag slung crossways over his body. "But it's fucking creepy how much she looks like Abby."

I rub at a tense spot between my brows. "So you've said, and I'm getting tired of hearing it." I sigh. "She's not Abby. She's her own person. And I happen to care about her a lot."

"I already guessed that." He plonks his jean-clad butt down on the seat in front of my desk.

I'm betting he's the current topic of gossip out on the floor. It's not every day they see a green-spikey-haired punk in grubby jeans, a rocker tee, and worn leather jacket roaming the corridors around here.

"You wouldn't have asked me to look into this if you didn't have feelings for her." He pulls some papers out of his bag.

"What have you discovered?" I ask, wanting to move this along.

"Her father's cancer is advanced."

The first thing I did last night when I overheard Margaret Ann discussing the fundraiser, and the reason for it, was call Xavier, asking him to find out what he could about Henry Alexander's medical condition. All I knew was he'd had a stroke that meant he was now confined to a wheelchair.

"Demi said he's been told he only has a few months to live."

Empathy washes over his face as he rifles through a few documents. "That's what the consultant's report says." He hands me a few sheets of paper. "I copied all his medical files and charts. You should ask Rick to take a look at it. He might be at dinner on Sunday."

"I can't ask him there. Demi is coming with me," I admit, crossing one leg over my knee.

"It's serious between you?" He looks somewhat surprised.

"It's new, but I think it could be."

A genuine smile graces his mouth. "Good for you, dude. I hope it works out."

"What else did you discover from Henry's medical files," I ask, deliberately not commenting on his statement.

"There is an experimental drug trial that might benefit him, but it's pricey, and after going through his finances, it's clear that's a no-go."

"That's why she's fundraising," I murmur, more to myself. I pin sharp eyes on Xavier. "How much is participation in the trial?"

"Two hundred K."

"Send me all the details and details of his bank account."

"What are you going to do?"

"What do you think?" I scoff.

"Wow. You must really dig this chick."

I flip him the bird. "What else do I need to know?"

"Demi is up to her eyeballs in debt. She's got loans coming out of her ears."

"Could you update me with less cliché usage?"

Now, it's his turn to flip me off. "She topped up her student loans to help with her father's medical expenses. Her salary barely covers the mortgage and the household bills."

"Send me her bank details as well."

"You're going to clear all her shit too, huh?"

My jaw tightens. "She's partly in this mess because of my father. Henry should not have been let go. There was no brain damage and no reason why he couldn't have continued to perform his role. We have flexible working and remote working policies in operation he could've availed of. If he was still an employee, he would have full private medical coverage. She wouldn't have had to drop out of school, and she wouldn't be drowning in debt."

"You'd never have met her then."

"Thanks for pointing that out, Captain Obvious."

"She deserves a fucking medal for putting up with your grumpy ass," he adds, chewing on a toothpick he removes from the pocket of his jacket.

"She happens to like my grumpy ass."

"Guess there's no accounting for taste."

"How *is* Hunt these days?"

He grins. "Hot as fuck. And the biggest pain in my ass."

I snort. "Literally, huh?"

Xavier leans forward, propping his elbows on the desk. "Charlie boy, are you asking if I'm a bottom?" His eyes glint mischievously.

I crank out a laugh. "As if anyone needs to ask that question!"

He pouts. "Now, you're just being rude." He folds his arms across his chest, huffing.

"Relax, dude. I'm just yanking your... Yeah, let's not go there." This conversation is quickly sinking to the gutter, and I want to maintain focus. I clear my throat and sit up straighter. "I'm guessing Lauder and Hunt will be at dinner?"

He drops the pout, relaxing back into the chair. "Yeah. You can watch Jackson and Drew snarking at one another. It's my new favorite hobby."

What the hell am I getting myself into? "I can hardly wait."

He hands me a sealed envelope. "I've got to get back to work. Thought it best to let you go through this in your own time."

"What is it?"

"The reason why your father was such an asshole to Demi's dad." He stands. "Just so you know, it might upset you a little."

Bile travels up my throat. "Thanks, man."

He nods. "Anytime." He strolls toward the door. "See you, Sunday, boy scout."

I throw my stapler at his retreating back, but it bounces off the door, crashing to the ground, as he exits my office, whistling under his breath.

I arrive at Demi's house early on Sunday because I want to talk with her father. Henry opens the door, grinning widely when he sees me standing on his front porch with a massive bouquet of flowers nestled against my chest. "Charlie. It's so good to see you. Come on in."

I wait for him to pivot in his wheelchair before entering the house, closing the door behind me.

"I assume Demi isn't expecting you yet because she's still out in her studio."

"Studio?" I inquire, following him into a homey living room.

"She didn't mention she hand paints furniture?"

I shake my head as he gestures toward the couch. "We're still getting to know one another."

"So I hear."

I put the bouquet down on the small mahogany table before taking a seat on the couch across from him. "She's mentioned me then."

"She has. There are no secrets between me and my little girl."

His eyes well up, and I scan his face, noticing how much he has changed. His skin is ashen, his eyes are sunken and blood-shot, and his clothes hang off his frame. He was always lean, but he's lost a lot of weight, and he's near skeletal now.

"I was very sorry to hear about the cancer, sir."

"When your time is up, your time is up." He breaks out in a coughing fit, and I move to his side, grabbing a handful of tissues and giving them to him. When the fit passes, he reaches for his glass of water, holding it in shaking hands. "I'm just sorry to be leaving my princess all alone," he says, continuing where we left off. "But I can't deny my joy at being reunited with my Luana."

"I know about her," I admit, sitting back down. "I know she's the reason my father treated you so disrespectfully."

He doesn't look shocked that I've uncovered the truth. "I haven't told Demi because it's been irrelevant."

"Until my father shafted you. He had no right to treat you

like that, and I'm shocked, because that's not the man I thought him to be."

"Your father was a good man, Charlie, but he was human, just like the rest of us. I forgave him a long time ago."

"How?" I don't understand how he could be so charitable.

"Because he did more good than harm. And he gave me a job after my wife died, allowing me to stay close to home so I could be here for Demi. I never forgot that kindness."

"You're a bigger man than me, Henry."

"Oh, I doubt that's true. You sell yourself short, young man. My sources tell me you're continuing your father's volunteer work."

I nod. "I go to the women's refuge center every Monday evening."

I found out a lot of things I didn't know about my father after he passed. Like how he donated huge sums to charities who work to protect women and children who have been subjected to abuse and neglect. I learned he and my mother volunteered at the local women's refuge center every Monday for years, and I didn't hesitate to step into their shoes. I know why my father did it, and I share some of the same guilt and remorse.

"You're a good man, Charlie, and it helps to know Demi has you in her life."

"Charlie?" Demi comes into the room wearing a pair of paint-splattered jean dungarees over a black tank and stained white sneakers. Her hair is tied up in a messy bun perched on top of her head, and she hasn't a scrap of makeup on her face. A glittery gold streak paints one cheek.

I've never seen her look more beautiful, and I know now I've fallen hard.

"Hey." I stand, pressing a kiss to the top of her head. "I know I'm early, but I was hoping to talk to you both."

Her brow furrows. "Is everything okay?"

I take her hand, tugging her down beside me. "I hope it will be." I lace my fingers in hers, staring into the warm depths of her eyes. A moment passes between us as we stare at one another. My heart thuds behind my rib cage, and blood courses through my veins. Butterflies swarm my chest, and the longer I stare at her, the more I realize that I'm head over heels in love with Demi Alexander.

It's been a slow, gradual incline and then a sudden unexpected fall into this heady feeling.

"You look at my daughter the same way I used to look at her mother," Henry says.

His words break our emotional eye lock, and we both turn to look at him.

"With an understanding that everything begins and ends with her," he adds, smiling. I'm grateful he seems to approve and that he's not wheeling off in search of a bat to chase me out of the house.

If he knew all the stuff I've been involved in, he'd do more than take a bat to me.

"It does," I agree, looking at Demi.

Her stunning smile lights up her whole face, and when she scoots in closer, I open my arm for her, tucking her into my side, uncaring if she gets paint on me.

"What was it you wanted to discuss?" Henry asks. "I know you youngsters are in a rush."

Demi glances at the clock on the wall. "Shoot. I need to get my butt in the shower."

"Wait a sec," I say, holding her tighter against me. "You need to hear this too."

She shares a look with her father.

"The company will cover the costs so you can participate in

the experimental drug trial," I say, just putting it out there with no fanfare.

Demi's eyes widen in shock. "How do you—"

"Did you really think I wouldn't find out?"

Henry shakes his head. "I appreciate the generous offer, son, but I'll have to decline."

"I thought you might say that." I stare into his eyes. "This isn't charity, sir. This is what you are owed. Your employment should never have been terminated. We both know that. Consider it a bonus on your severance package."

"I can't accept, Charlie."

"Why not, Dad?" Demi beseeches.

"Because it's not right, Demi. Charlie is not responsible for the decisions his father made, and I left of my own free will. No one forced my hand."

"If you won't accept it for yourself," I say. "Accept it for Demi. Give her as much time with you as possible."

He's wavering, but he's still not there.

"I could have done this much differently, and I was going to at first. I was going to make an anonymous donation and ask the hospital to advise you that you had been awarded the funds, but I'm sick of secrets and lies. I wanted to come in here and tell you to your face that we're doing this because it's the right thing to do. For you and your daughter."

I turn my face to Demi. Silent tears are streaming down her face. "Your daughter's happiness is of huge importance to me." I look over at Henry again. "As I know it is to you too. That's why you're going to accept."

His Adam's apple jumps in his throat. "I don't know what to say, Charlie. This is—"

"Just say yes."

He nods, and Demi jumps up, rushing to hug her father. "Thank you, Charlie," he says in a choked voice.

"One other thing you should know." I rub my hands over my black jeans. "And this one is on me. I paid off your mortgage, cleared your medical bills, and your student loans are no more, Demi."

Tears leak out of her eyes. "Oh my God, Charlie. You shouldn't have done that," she croaks.

I rise. "I want to take care of you, starting with easing your financial burden."

She launches herself at me, half-crying, half-laughing, stepping on her tiptoes to peck my lips. "You are crazy, Charlie Barron, and I'm crazy about you."

Chapter Thirteen
Demi

"I'm still in shock," I admit from the passenger seat of Charlie's Land Rover. "And I should probably be mad that you did all that, but I'm too freaking happy right now to care."

He slides his hand across the console, squeezing my fingers. "It's only money, and you should have come to me about it."

"It's only money," I harrumph, shaking my head. "Only someone with endless pots of money could say something like that."

"I can't help that I come from a wealthy family, and it's not something I'll ever apologize for, but what good is money if you can't help your loved ones out in times of need?"

My heart skips a beat at his words, the memory of the gorgeous flowers he brought for me, and his extremely thoughtful, generous gesture, and I've a sudden urge to tell him I love him.

I stare out the window in a bit of a daze as the realization dawns.

I'm in love with him.

And I think I have been for some time.

It's been creeping up on me without me noticing.

"Hey. Where'd you go?" he asks, squeezing my fingers again.

"I'm here." I stretch across the console to press a feather-soft kiss to his cheek. "Thank you. Thank you so much. You've no idea how much this means."

"I'm glad I was able to help. Your dad is a great guy, and he deserves a fighting chance."

I gulp over the painful lump in my throat as I slump back in my seat. "He does, and I hope it works, but it's not a miracle cure."

"You're not alone in this, Demi. I'm here for you, and whatever happens, I will be right by your side."

***

"Are you sure I'm dressed okay?" I ask for the umpteenth time as we climb out of the car. There are a bunch of other cars in the driveway and a motorbike. I glance up at the sophisticated two-story modern building, composed of cream stone, cherrywood panels, and large glass windows, in awe. It's a beautiful home, and I'll bet the inside is to die for. While it's no mansion, it clearly cost a pretty penny. Money seems to be in plentiful supply in the circles Charlie mixes in.

"You're perfect." Charlie kisses me softly, claiming my sole attention. "Stop worrying. They will love you."

I retrieve the bag with the chocolate cake I baked and the hand-painted picture frame from the back seat of the car. I wanted to bring wine, but we didn't have any at home, and there isn't spare cash for luxuries like that.

Well, there wasn't before, but there is now, thanks to Charlie.

The urge to tell him I love him rides me hard, but I bite my tongue because the revelation is new and I haven't forgotten the need to protect my heart.

Charlie takes the bag, and I smooth a hand down over my knee-length pink-and-purple-patterned dress. It's my favorite dress. Casual but still dressy and comfortable. I've teamed it with a soft pink cardigan and silver ballet pumps. My hair is long and loose, and the only makeup I have on is some mascara, some blush, and gloss on my lips.

Charlie takes my hand, and I hope he can't feel how clammy my palm is or hear how anxiously my heart is beating in my chest.

"Breathe, babe," he says when we reach the door. "You'll like them."

He rings the doorbell, and it's opened a minute later by a beaming Abby. She's wearing a gorgeous fitted knee-length red dress with black ballet pumps, and her hair is styled similarly to mine. "I'm so happy you're here!" She hugs Charlie first and then me. "Welcome to our home. Come in," she adds, stepping aside to let us enter. "Everyone is back here."

We follow her along a wide airy hallway, our shoes squelching off the cream porcelain-tiled floor. The walls are adorned with tons of family photos, and I'm happy I made her the picture frame now because it seems like the perfect gift.

Abby leads us into a large open-plan space that is stylishly decorated yet warm and inviting at the same time. There is a massive kitchen with stainless steel appliances and white and gray gloss cupboards at the rear of the space. The kitchen overlooks a manicured back garden with a pool and patio area.

A long dining table occupies prime real estate in the center of the space. An industrial-type light fitting hangs over the length of the rustic table, illuminating the picture-perfect settings. The table seats twelve and there's a place setting in front of every chair, confirming we have a full house.

My nerves ramp up another notch.

Abby steers us to the left, to the main living space, where everyone is congregated. A bunch of strapping guys are chatting in a circle. Behind them, on one of the long white leather couches, three women are deep in conversation. One of the women looks to be around our age, and the other two women are older.

My heart rate picks up as adrenaline courses through my body. I grip Charlie's hand so tight, it's a wonder there's any blood flowing to it.

"Everyone. Charlie and Demi are here," Abby says, announcing us to the room. I can scarcely hear over the thrumming of blood in my ears. As if in slow-motion, everyone stops talking, and every head turns in our direction.

A deathly quiet descends over the room as everyone stares at me. Eyes widen, and incredulous looks are exchanged. I shuffle awkwardly on my feet, clinging to Charlie's side, as panic inches up my throat.

Charlie bristles beside me. He thrusts the bag at Abby. "This was a mistake." A muscle pops in his jaw. "You're a bunch of assholes." He glares at the guys before looking down at me. "C'mon. We're leaving."

"Don't," Abby pleads, her gaze dancing between Charlie and her husband.

I recognize Kaiden Anderson from photos I've seen of him online. Although, the photos haven't done him justice because he's way hotter in the flesh. As my gaze quickly flits around the faces, I recognize most everyone in the room, for the same reason, with the exception of the younger woman and one of the older women.

"Charlie, wait." Kaiden steps forward, and Abby's shoulders visibly relax. "We don't mean to be rude. It's just a shock." He steps right up to me as Abby hands the bag off to the woman I recognize as her mother. Kaiden extends his hand. "It's nice to meet you, Demi."

I shake his hand, cringing at how sweaty my palm must feel against his cool one. "Thank you for inviting me."

"Forgive us," he adds, trying hard not to stare at me. "Abby said you two looked alike, but it's still a shock." He glances at Charlie briefly. Charlie is like a brick beside me, and I lean in closer to him, offering him silent support as much as I need to take it from him.

Drew Manning comes forward as Abby slides in under Kaiden's arm. He smiles, but it's a little off. "The resemblance is uncanny."

Charlie is seconds away from imploding, and I wish the ground would open up and swallow me.

"Get over yourselves, peeps," Xavier says, strolling confidently to my free side, wrapping his arm around me. "There's actually a logical explanation for this."

All eyeballs turn in his direction, and I'm glad the attention has been diverted.

"There is?" Abby inquires, her brows climbing to her hairline.

"You're related," he tosses out.

I blink repeatedly, wondering if I misheard him although that would explain a lot. Abby smiles as her eyes find mine.

"What?" Charlie snaps. "Why am I only hearing this now?"

"Why are *you*?" Abby pokes Charlie in the chest, grabbing my hand and pulling me toward her. 'Why are *we*?" She eyeballs Xavier. "What do you know, oh wise one." I appreciate her attempt at humor because the tension is suffocating at this point.

"Why don't we all sit down and have a drink while Xavier fills us in," Abby's mom says, smiling at everyone. She leans forward, kissing me on the cheek. "You're most welcome, Demi. I'm Olivia. Drew and Abby's Mom."

"It's lovely to meet you."

She palms Charlie's face. "It's been too long, Charlie. You're family. Never forget that."

"Olivia." He kisses her cheek. "It's good to see you." He accepts a hug from the other older lady. "You too, Sylvia. You're looking well."

"As are you." She extends her hand to me. "Pleasure to meet you, Demi."

"Welp," Abby says, turning us around to face the only two guys I haven't interacted with. "Where are your manners?" She points at Jackson Lauder and Sawyer Hunt. "Come say hi to Charlie's girl."

Charlie slides up behind me, none too subtly pulling me away from Abby. He wraps his arms around me, pressing his body up against me.

"Pissing on your territory, Barron?" Jackson says, grinning over my shoulder at my boyfriend.

"It's a reminder to watch those legendary wandering hands of yours," Charlie retorts.

"You don't need to worry," Sawyer says, smiling at me as he addresses Charlie. "Jackson has his panties twisted into knots over Nessa. He's only got eyes for her."

"Shut your Goddamned mouth, Hunt, or I'll shut it for you," Jackson spits, all humor instantly fading from his eyes. His hands clench into fists at his sides. He faces me, making an effort to relax his facial muscles. A wicked glint races across his eyes. "If you ever grow tired of Barron, look me up. I've been searching for my own Abby clone."

"Jackson!" Abby screeches, as Charlie thrusts his fist out

and punches Lauder in the nose. Jackson is caught off guard, and he takes a tumble.

"Was that really necessary?" Kaiden drawls, narrowing his eyes at Charlie.

"Yes," Charlie hisses. "I expect to get shade for the shit I've pulled, but leave Demi out of it."

My heart swells at his obvious protectiveness. I take Charlie's hand in mine, inspecting his clenched knuckles, as Hunt hauls a semi-contrite Jackson up off the floor, and Sylvia brushes past us on her way to the kitchen.

"Happy families," the strange woman says, smiling as she sidles up to me. "I'm Shandra. A friend of Abby's." She casts a lingering look at Drew before quickly lowering her eyes.

"Are they always like this?" I ask.

"Never a dull moment," Drew says, coming up and offering me a glass of wine. "I didn't introduce myself earlier. I'm Drew. Abby's twin."

I know, because I've snooped on all of you online. For the first time, it feels wrong that I did. But it was months ago, and I had no idea I'd end up meeting all of them one day.

"Hey." I smile at him, feeling overwhelmed.

"Charlie." Drew slaps my boyfriend on the back. "Glad you're here, man."

After Jackson makes groveling apologies, we all get comfortable on the couches to hear what Xavier has to say.

"You okay?" Charlie whispers in my ear. We're tucked up against one another on the couch with Abby and Drew on my other side. I nod, clinging to him a little closer. "I'm sorry about that, but at least, we got it over and done with."

I press a kiss to his cheek. "Thank fuck, because that was one of the most embarrassing experiences of my life," I whisper.

He quietly chuckles. "I know the feeling." At least, he seems to have loosened up.

"Spit it out, Daniels. We don't have all day," Kaiden says from his perch on the arm of the couch.

"Kaiden." Olivia tut-tuts. "Don't be rude."

"Sorry, Mom." He blows her a kiss. "Whenever you're ready, your lordship." He smirks at Xavier.

"I prefer Star Lord," Xavier quips. "It's got a nicer ring to it."

"You're no Chris Pratt," Drew says, grinning.

"The dinner is getting cold," Hunt says, rolling his eyes and sighing. "So, sometime this century would be nice, please."

"No foreplay in front of the oldies," Jackson says, leaning back against the couch, smirking, and I'm guessing there's some inside joke at play. I make a mental note to ask Charlie later.

But the banter is great, and it's just what's needed after a very tense start to our afternoon. There's a lovely vibe among the crew and a genuine camaraderie I'm now enjoying. I also love, and appreciate, how everyone has forgotten the little spat. I grew up with a father who never let disagreements fester. If we had beef with one another, we aired that shit and quickly moved on. I respect and expect straight shooting from the people in my life.

"For the love of all things holy." Abby throws her arms into the air. "Everyone, shut up and let Xavier speak."

The room instantly mutes, and I share a grin with Abby, loving her strength and the obvious loyalty she commands from everyone here. I watch her husband stare at her with so much adoration and admiration it almost takes my breath away. She's a lucky woman to be loved so fiercely.

Drew clasps Abby's hand, smiling warmly at me, as we prepare for whatever Xavier is about to tell us. Abby takes my hand in hers, and it feels surreal to be here, with the woman I've feared and felt inconsequential against, liking her and wanting to get to know her better. The world truly works in mysterious ways.

"Your grandmothers were sisters," Xavier says, just putting it out there. "Paternal on the Hearst side, maternal on your side, Demi."

"So, my mom's mom was the sister of Abby and Drew's dad's mom?" I say, working it out, out loud.

"Michael's adopted mom or birth mom?" Drew asks.

"Birth mom," Xavier says, pulling a crumpled photo out of his back pocket. He hands it to Abby. "No idea why her family didn't take Michael in when he was orphaned."

"They probably knew he was the devil's spawn and wanted nothing to do with him," Drew says, and my eyes pop wide. There is so much I don't know but I hope to discover in time. His statement is met with silence, and no one jumps in to refute his claim, which says a lot.

"Holy shit," Abby says, running her finger over the picture.

Charlie leans over my shoulder while Drew and Kai lean over Abby's.

"Were they twins?" I ask, because the two younger girls in the picture look identical.

"Yep," Xavier confirms. "And you two are the image of them. It's a little creepy."

"At least, we have an explanation for it," Abby says, beaming at me as she flings her arms around me. "I can't believe we're cousins."

"I know. It's crazy." I still haven't wrapped my head around it, and I doubt I will for some time.

Charlie kisses the top of my head, as Drew leans over, grinning. "Welcome to the family, Demi."

Chapter Fourteen
Demi

"Are you still in shock?" Charlie asks as we are seated side by side around the dinner table. Abby, Olivia, Sylvia, and Shandra cooked a spectacular feast, and everything I've tasted is melt-in-the-mouth good.

"For sure," I truthfully admit, putting my fork down, unable to eat another morsel. "I've grown up with no family because both my parents were only children and their folks died before I had a chance to know them. I never met any extended family, and Dad never talked about any."

"Well, you have family now," Charlie says, linking his fingers in mine under the table.

"Dad will be happy," I admit, because I know how much he hates that he's leaving me all alone. Now, I have Charlie and Abby and Drew.

"You should talk to your dad about the past," he suggests, and I eye him circumspectly. I'm sensing there is something he's not telling me, but before I can pry, Drew speaks.

"Did you receive your invitation to the elite ball?" Drew asks Charlie from across the table.

"I did." Charlie tosses his napkin on the table. "They sent Mom one too." His jaw tightens, and fire blazes in his eyes.

"She's the widow of a descendant of a founding father," Olivia says. "Of course, they would send her one. We both got one too," she adds, glancing at Sylvia.

"I thought the elite looked down their noses at women," Xavier says, popping a piece of carrot in his mouth and chewing noisily.

"They do," Olivia agrees. "But with Michael and Charles gone, and Christian still on the run from the authorities, their responsibilities pass to us until our children assume full membership within the order."

"Which is something William Hamilton will no doubt address at the ball now he's been voted into the vacant president's chair," Kaiden says. His arm is around Abby's shoulder, and he's absently playing with strands of her hair. I've noticed they are always subtly touching one another, and it's obvious they are crazy in love.

"What are you going to do about Joaquin and Harley?" Olivia asks.

Kaiden's nostrils flare. "There is no way they are attending that ball or accepting the invitation to train at Parkhurst. Rick and I will cover in Atticus's absence, but hell will freeze over before we let our younger brothers get pulled into things." He scrubs a hand over his prickly jawline. "Rick is talking to a guy today. It's why he couldn't be here. He's one of the few senior elite members who wants to use this opportunity to restructure the order for good. He's on the reorganizing committee, so we're hoping he's a sympathetic ear."

"What do we know about the new president?" Drew asks Xavier.

"William Hamilton is the eldest son of a founding father from Texas. Family comes from oil. He's married with two daughters. He was one of the men swindled by Christian and one of the very few who publicly opposed Michael Hearst for president. He has spoken out about the archaic rules and asserted his desire to modernize the elite."

"Sounds squeaky clean," Jackson says. "I'm not buying it."

"Neither did we," Sawyer says, putting his glass down. "So, we did some investigating on the darknet—"

"And this guy makes Michael Hearst look like the fairy fucking godmother," Xavier finishes.

"Do you have to cut across me every time?" Sawyer purses his lips, drilling a look at Xavier.

"No need to get your panties in a bunch. We play for the same team, remember?" Xavier smirks, and everyone catches the innuendo.

Ah, now it makes sense. They're together or hooking up, or there's some history between them.

"Just tell us what you discovered," Abby says. "And keep your foreplay confined to the bedroom."

Sawyer glares at Abby, and Kaiden glares at him.

Charlie winks at me, grinning. He presses his mouth to my ear. "This shit happens all the time. I've kind of missed it."

I grin at him as Xavier clears his throat and finishes explaining. "It's the usual elite bullshit. Professional businessman with legit businesses that are all a front for a host of illegal activities, but this guy is into everything."

"And we mean *everything*," Sawyer says, jumping in and taking the mantle. Xavier meets Sawyer's smug grin with an amused one, further incensing him. A muscle ticks in Sawyer's jaw as he speaks. "Drugs, guns, sex, and it's a global operation worth *billions*."

"This is like déjà vu," Abby says, leaning back into her husband's chest.

"Round two is due to begin," Drew agrees. "And we need to get battle ready."

"He's going to be careful," Charlie says, rubbing his hand up and down my thigh. "Because the FBI is still sniffing around, right?"

Kaiden nods. "Yes, but, according to Keven Kennedy, the investigation is winding down. They've gotten some high-profile arrests, and they found the girls Hearst had kidnapped and put an end to his sex ring, but we all know that's only the tip of the iceberg. However, the elite has covered their tracks well and planned for this eventuality. They gave them some scapegoats, and the powers that be are happy with that."

"Sounds fishy," Charlie says.

"One hundred percent," Drew agrees. "Keven is convinced they have powerful allies in the FBI and government who are guiding this behind the scenes."

"This shitshow is about to start up again, and none of us know how it's going to affect us," Abby says.

"We thought for sure they would kick us out because of the stunt we pulled, but they seem determined to reel us back in," Drew says with a frown. "Which can't be good."

"No shit, Sherlock," Jackson says, rolling his eyes. Drew scowls at him.

"They're not going to let our interference go unpunished," Kaiden agrees. "Not when it brought the FBI down on them."

I'm completely lost, and I don't know what they are talking about, but I'm picking up on the anxious energy in the room, and I know it's nothing good.

Abby's eyes land on mine, and then, she moves her gaze to Charlie. "Have you explained any of this to Demi?"

"Not yet," he admits, squeezing my thigh.

"Well, you need to do it sooner than later. Definitely before the ball so she's prepared for what she's walking into."

Charlie lifts his hand from my thigh, running it through his hair. He's let it grow out in recent months, and it's much longer on top now. When he's at the office, he wears it slicked back and neat, but today, he hasn't put product in, and I adore the tumble of messy waves falling over his forehead and into his eyes. He's like a hotter version of Shawn Mendes, and that's saying a lot because Shawn is hot as fuck.

But my man is hotter.

Tension oozes from Charlie, and he looks pained as he glances at me. "I'm not sure you should attend," he tells me.

"Demi is in your life, Charlie," Abby says, leaning forward and placing her elbows on the table. "We need to start thinking about protection. I can help with self-defense and gun lessons." She looks to me, and I nod, because I don't have any issue with that. "We have a month until the ball. That's enough time to get you ready."

Charlie shifts in his seat, averting his eyes as he reluctantly nods. His chest heaves, and his expression is troubled. A lump forms at the base of my throat. I don't like the vibes he's emitting, and I'm determined to get to the bottom of this when we leave.

The conversation turns more casual after that, and the guys clear the table around the women as we drink wine and talk. The girls go out of their way to include me, and a warmth spreads over my chest, eliminating the chill left behind from the previous discussion.

After everything is cleared away, Abby nabs me and Drew and pulls us out to the sunnier side of the living room. "We need a photo," she says, positioning herself in between me and her brother and sliding her arm around my waist. "For my gorgeous new photo frame."

Kaiden snaps a few pics, sending them to my cell. "I'll print out a copy for you too," Abby assures me, looping her arm through mine. And when I'm hugging her goodbye a few hours later, I hug her tight, ecstatic to have her in my life. Go figure.

"Do you need to get home, or could you come back to my place for a while? There are some things we need to discuss," Charlie says while backing out of the driveway.

I wave at Abby, Drew, and Kaiden, watching as they withdraw into the house and shut the door.

"I want to have that conversation," I agree, glad he put it out there so bluntly and that he's not trying to shield anything from me. "Let me message Xena and check she's okay to keep Dad company for a few hours." I tap out a text to my friend, and she responds affirmatively. "We're good."

My eyes almost bug out of my head when we pull up in front of Charlie's home fifteen minutes later. "Holy shit. You live *here*?" I gawk at the impressive mansion set on the grounds of a sprawling estate. "How many rooms do you have?"

"I honestly couldn't tell you." He pulls into a garage at the back of the property, maneuvering his Land Rover into a spot beside a silver Bentley. There are at least ten other cars in here. A mix of sports cars, top-end luxury cars, and SUVS, and if I added it up, I'm guessing the cost of these cars outweighs the cost of my house.

He helps me out of the car, escorting me into the house through a side door in the garage. He gives me a quick guided tour, but it still takes a half hour to show me the lower level because this place is massive.

I cannot fathom the enormity of his wealth.

It's one thing to know he's rich but quite another to be confronted by it in such a visible way.

I also can't believe he lives in this gorgeous, rambling mansion all by himself. I don't think I'd like it.

He brings me down to a basement room that is obviously his man lair, and it's the most casual, comfortable room he's shown me to date. It has a fully stocked bar, a pool table, top-of-the-line stereo system, and a wall-mounted TV screen that is almost the size of the screen in the Rydeville movie theater.

He pops a beer, the first alcohol he's drank all day, and then, he makes me a mean gin cocktail. We kick off our shoes and snuggle up on the couch, sipping our drinks and just enjoying each other's company. After a few minutes, we put our drinks down on the coffee table and turn so we're facing one another.

"How much do you know about Parkhurst and the elite organization," he asks, and I appreciate he's getting straight to it.

"As much as I've heard on the news or found online. I know Parkhurst was the headquarters for the elite, but the public perception was that of a private medical and pharmaceutical company." He nods. "And I know they made several high-profile arrests. Former elite members who were involved in wide-ranging criminal activities."

"All that is correct," Charlie says, tucking my hair behind my ears. "But that's not the half of it. The elite is an organiza-tion that was started in the eighteen hundreds by our forefa-thers. As generations passed, membership was inherited by the children in each family. There is no choice. It is something we all must accept as tradition. Descendants of founding fathers in every state hold most seniority within the elite, but there is an inner circle, made up of other important members of rich society who are the backbone of the organization."

"It sounds like fiction," I admit.

"You have no idea." He shakes his head. "It's the most powerful organization in the world, and its reach spans multiple countries. Members are important figureheads in busi-ness and government. Fraud and corruption are commonplace as are illegal activities. What you heard at Abby and Kai's house today is not unusual. These men have their fingers in several cookie jars, and they believe they are above the law. Usually, they are. But Abby and the others threw a wrench in the works. It's a story in itself, and one I'll tell you another day, but they almost succeeded in bringing the elite to their knees. It's a first, and I doubt the elite will leave themselves open to exposure again."

"Before Epstein, I might have accused you of blowing smoke, but I know this shit exists."

"It does, and we are in the thick of it. The organization is restructuring, and I must play a part whether I want to or not. Kai, Rick, Abby, and Drew are in the same boat. It's what I've been training for since I was ten."

"Training?" I rub a hand along the back of my neck. "What do you mean?"

He audibly gulps. "Drew, Trent, and I have been going to Parkhurst annually to prepare for the time when we would become full members of the elite and assume our birthright."

"Trent was Sylvia's son? The bomb killed him, right?" I ask, remembering what I've read.

"Someone has done their homework," he says, and I blush.

"I was curious about Abby," I truthfully admit. "So, I read everything I could get my hands on."

He kisses me softly. "I'm impressed, and maybe, you're more ready for this world than I think." He pulls me into his arms, and I reposition myself on his lap with my legs stretched out to the side. "Trent used to be one of my closest friends, but he was a bastard, and at the time he died, we were enemies. The bomb didn't kill him. Jackson did."

I startle, jumping on his lap as shock rams into me.

"It was self-defense," Charlie explains, "and I have zero remorse for his death, because he tried to kill Abby."

"But you took the bullet instead," I say, working it all out in my mind.

"Yes." He clasps my face in his warm palms. "And I hope you know I'd take a bullet for you too."

A shudder works its way through me. "I hope you never have to."

"So do I, but the world I inhabit is a dangerous world, and you need to understand what you are walking into if you decide to continue dating me."

Now, it's my turn to cup his face. "There is no decision to be made. It's already done. I'm yours, Charlie. Whatever is coming, we will face it together because I'm all in, and there is nothing you can say that will make me change my mind."

Chapter Fifteen
Charlie

I want to believe that so badly, but I'm terrified she'll want nothing to do with me when she finds out the stuff I've done. I'm not giving her specifics, because some of it is too heinous to speak out loud, but I need to tell her enough so she understands the kind of man I am. "I hope you still feel like that after you find out what I've done."

"Hey." She pins me with those luscious eyes, emotion brimming behind them. "I know there's a good guy behind that asshole front you like to wear."

"I've done a lot of bad shit, Demi. Things I can't take back."

"Tell me about this training. Tell me what they forced you to do."

I hold her more tightly, nuzzling into her neck and breathing her in as I prepare to tell her things I've told no one before. "Training was two-fold. Preparing us to take control of our family business and preparing us to be men of the elite. That involved a lot of physical tasks." Acid crawls up my throat. "I lost my virginity at thirteen to an older woman who had been assigned as my sexual mentor at age twelve."

Her jaw slackens. "What the what?"

"Sex has always been a purely physical act for me, and I've, ah, got certain tastes."

"Like what?" Interest piques on her face.

"Bondage. Domination and other kinks." I don't want to scare her off by revealing the true extent of my depraved sexual fantasies—especially the ones involving her.

"You say that like it'll send me running away screaming."

"I doubt you're used to the kind of sex I crave."

She repositions herself on my lap until she's straddling me. She tilts my chin up. "I'm not, but that doesn't mean I'm closed off. I'm open to exploring my sexuality with you, and maybe, you could be open to exploring intimacy with me?"

God, she's sweet but so misguided. "I don't know how else to be." I brush my fingers across her cheek. "I want to experience intimacy with you, but I'm not sure I know how."

"We'll figure it out together. None of that is a deal breaker, so what else do I need to know?"

"I've killed people, Demi. Never by choice and not always out of necessity. The elite live by their own set of rules, and there were times when we were instructed to kill for no reason but to prove they could control us and freely take lives."

Shock splays across her face as she stares at me.

I go on, needing to purge this. "Some of the initiation rituals were violent and brutal, and it was a kill or be killed scenario. I made my first kill at fourteen, and I had nightmares for months after. Sometimes, when I close my eyes at night, I still see his face." I squeeze my eyes shut for a moment. "The things I've done haunt me."

"That proves you're a good person."

"I've just admitted I like to hurt women during sex, and I've killed people, and you think I'm a good person?!" I snap, more angry at myself than her.

She grabs my face firmly, staring deep into my eyes. "Don't act dumb. You know what I'm saying and why I'm saying it. If you were a cold-blooded pervert killer, you'd feel no guilt, no remorse, and show no desire to change." She runs her finger along my lower lip. "I'm not going to lie. I'm shocked and sickened, but I also understand you were a kid, and they forced you to do things no kid should ever have to do." Tears pool in her eyes. "Don't you see how strong you are to have survived that? And you still know what's right from wrong. That speaks volumes, Charlie."

"I've stood by and watched the elite abuse kidnapped kids. I've seen those poor innocents drugged to their eyeballs and then callously disposed of when they were no longer of any use. I've watched elite members pass their wives around like they're candy. I've turned a blind eye when those women cried out in pain and shame. I've ignored the criminal activities driven by morally corrupt men with a single-minded thirst for power."

"You were a kid, Charlie." She grips my chin in her soft hands. "You probably had PTSD. And it's not like you could've done anything to stop it. You were a kid, and they were powerful men with no moral compass. If you'd tried to help, they would have killed you."

She's grasping this more easily than I expected, and I don't think I've given her enough credit even though she has proven her inner strength to me over and over. "I haven't been a kid for a long time, Demi." I swallow a knot in my throat.

"That saddens me," she says. "I had no idea you existed in such a dark world. No idea those kinds of things were going on so close to home."

"If you hadn't met me, you still wouldn't know."

"Living in blissful ignorance is no way to live," she says. "And I happen to be pretty fond of your grumpy ass, so I'll take the trade-off."

I take her wrists in my hands, rubbing my thumbs back and forth across her velvety-soft skin. "Why are you still here? Why aren't you disgusted with me? Why aren't you leaving?"

She rests her forehead against mine. "You told me before that you see me. Well, I see you too, Charlie, and I like what I see." She eases back. "Unless you tell me you enjoy all the things you've done and seen, I'm going nowhere."

"I'm sickened by everything I've done and seen, and I want to put an end to it all. Not just for me but for my friends and future generations. The elite has got to be stopped once and for all."

"That's what the discussion was about at the table."

I nod. "We hoped we'd put an end to it before, but we should've known the elite would not go quietly. Now, they are more determined than ever. But so are we." Resolve flows through me. "We won't stop until their reign is ended."

***

The next few weeks pass by in a blur of activity. Work is busy because I'm project-managing the new regulatory system implementation and spearheading a new workplace culture initiative. Unfortunately, it means working closely with Corrinna Smith, our chief human relations officer. Her constant flirting is a major pain in my ass, so I purposely out my relationship with Demi at the same time I announce we are terminating the no-fraternization policy.

Corrinna didn't take kindly to it, and now, I'm persona non grata.

Win-win for me.

Demi and I have been dating up a storm, and the more I'm with her, the more I fall deeper in love. I still haven't told her yet, or taken her to my bed, because I'm trying to rein things in.

We've been making out like demons, and we've gone down on each other, *a lot*, but it hasn't progressed any further, because I haven't let it.

But I'm all out of patience, and I think Demi is too, so tonight is the night.

I light the candles resting atop the table in the kitchen just as the doorbell chimes. Butterflies swoop into my stomach as I race to the front door, eager to hold my girl in my arms.

"Hey, babe." I reel her in flush to my body, and her bag drops to the ground, as I dip her down low and plant a slow, passionate kiss on her lips.

"Wow. That's some greeting," she teases when we finally come up for air.

"I missed you." I scoop up her bag and deposit it in the hall. Closing the door, I take her hand, leading her toward the kitchen.

"You saw me at work today," she says, beaming at me.

"That was hours ago." I grip her hips, pushing her into the wall as we step into the kitchen. "And every second we're apart, my heart hurts." I press an openmouthed kiss to the underside of her jaw, delighting when she shivers.

"That was very romantic," she pants, thrusting her chest into mine.

"I need to up the romance stakes before I unleash the beast on you later."

Her entire body shudders underneath me, and I freeze. "If you're not ready, we—"

She slams her mouth down on mine, biting on my lower lip, and blood rushes straight to my cock. "I'm ready, Charlie. I'm more than ready. I haven't been laid since Christmas night, and I have the lady equivalent of blue balls."

I grin, sucking on her lower lip. "I'm so horny for you, babe, and I can't wait to bury myself balls deep inside you."

Her lust-drenched eyes meet mine. "So, what are we waiting for? Take me to your bedroom."

"What about dinner?"

"We can reheat it."

I need no further encouragement, dashing to the stove and turning the heat off in the oven, praying the lasagna is salvageable later. I throw a paper towel over the salad and garlic bread before jogging to her side and yanking her up into my arms. "Wrap your legs around me, babe, and hold on tight." She does as she's told, and I sprint through the house and up the stairs, peppering kisses on her face and her neck, while she giggles and writhes against me.

By the time we reach my bedroom, I'm sweaty and my cock is about to spontaneously combust. I drop her on my bed and drag a chair across the carpeted floor, positioning it in front of my bed. "Strip for me."

She bites on the corner of her lip, and her cheeks flush, but she doesn't protest, kneeling up on the bed as she slowly removes her clothing until she's only in her bra and panties.

"Come here," I demand, and she crawls into my lap.

I tug the cups of her bra down, rolling her neat pink nipples between my thumbs and forefingers. "Have you ever worn a nipple clamp?" I ask, already guessing the answer.

She shakes her head. "No, but I'm willing to try."

I pinch her nipples, and a guttural moan leaves her lips. "We can work up to it." I press wet kisses along her collarbone as I continue to tease her nipples.

"Okay," she readily agrees, her eyes flush with eagerness.

I unclasp her bra and fling it aside, kneading her firm breasts with both hands, before I dive in, laving, sucking, and nipping at her tits and her nipples until she's squirming on my lap and there's a damp patch on her pretty lace panties. "How would you feel about wearing a blindfold and being tied to my bed?" I ask, licking a path up through the valley of her tits.

"I'm up for that," she rasps in a breathy tone, and my cock strains against my zipper, desperate to get inside her already. I plant my mouth on hers and kiss her deeply. When my tongue slides into her mouth, I groan at the sensations flooding my body and the feel of her tongue wrangling with mine. We devour one another as she moans and wriggles on top of me, and I can't prolong this any longer.

Not unless I want to come in my pants for the first time in years.

"Sit on the bed with your back against the headboard."

She does as I command while I open the top drawer of my bedside table. I rummage through the myriad of sex toys, finding a black silk blindfold and matching silk ties.

I undress quickly, loving how her eyes trace over every inch of my skin and how her tongue darts out, wetting her lips, as her gaze lingers on my erect cock. I'm hard as steel and likely to inflict damage unless I exercise self-control and force myself to take it easy.

I don't want to hurt her.

Not ever.

And I need to restrain my natural urges so I don't push her too far too fast. To date, she is enthusiastic and willing, and I'm hoping, in time, she'll come to share my sexual desires. I crawl up the bed until I'm between her legs. "You trust me?"

"Completely."

I lean down and kiss her. "I love kissing you," I admit over her lips. "I could do it nonstop for all time."

"I never thought I could feel so much from just a kiss," she admits. "But I feel your kisses in every part of me. You make my body tingle all over, and I'm addicted to the feeling."

"I'm addicted to you." I ravish her mouth, grinding my

pelvis against hers as I hold her arms up over her head. "God, Demi. You make me crazy with desire."

With gentle slow movements, I tie her wrists to my bed, ensuring they are not too tight. Then, I slide the blindfold down over her head, positioning it carefully over her eyes. "Do they feel okay?"

"Perfect," she says in a sultry, breathy tone of voice. "I'm so turned on, Charlie."

"I'd like to prove that for myself," I tell her, grabbing the edge of her panties with my teeth and pulling them down her body with the help of my hands.

I kneel in front of her, taking in every gorgeous, precious inch of her. The beast roars silently, urging me to take everything, but I draw a deep breath, quelling my baser desires as I nudge her legs wide and part the folds of her bare pussy with my thumbs. "You are exquisite, Demi." I blow over her sensitive flesh, and she squirms on the bed. "Don't move." My fingers creep slowly up and down her thighs, brushing over her mound, but never quite touching her, until I can't bear to torture both of us any longer, and I lick a line along her slit with my tongue.

She cries out, and the sound is like music to my ears. I destroy her pussy and her clit with my tongue, my lips, and my fingers, and I've never tasted anything so tempting or so deliciously sweet. She orgasms fast, and I love how responsive she is. I milk every last drop of her arousal while she's panting and arching her back. "Charlie, please. I need you."

I slide my finger into her damp heat and then withdraw it, placing the tip against her ass. I nudge my finger in ever so slightly, and she gasps. "Has anyone ever fucked you here?" I ask.

"No." Her voice trembles.

"Your ass is mine." I'm aware how possessive my tone is. "Not tonight, but soon."

"Okay." She sounds less sure, and I park that topic to discuss another time.

"Do I need a condom?" I ask.

"I have the implant," she says, adding, "And I'm clean."

I press the length of my body down on top of her, kissing her quickly. "I am too, and I've only ever had sex one time without a condom."

Most of the elite men give zero fucks about contraception. The women—and men—they fuck are always tested for STDs, so they don't care. Unwanted pregnancies are the norm and swiftly dealt with. It disgusts me, and wearing condoms is my one big fuck you to the rules. The only exception is the night I lost my virginity. That was in front of an audience, and I couldn't refuse. But it was the last time I fucked a woman bare.

"I want to feel you on my naked flesh, Demi. I've never wanted to ride bareback with any other woman, but I badly want to with you."

"I'm okay with that. Just get in me already," she demands.

I bark out a laugh, lining my cock up at her entrance and slamming inside her in one fast move. She screams at the unexpectedness as I bend her legs back, pressing her knees into her chest. I fuck her relentlessly, pounding in and out of her like it's a competition and I need to go faster. Her tight walls hug my cock, and it's the most incredible feeling. I feel every inch of her heat as I thrust in and out of her, and every nerve ending on my body is on fire.

I worship her body with my hands, my lips, and my cock, and I'm drowning in everything Demi. I rip the blindfold from her face, needing to look at her as I slide in and out of her body. Her gaze locks on mine, and there's no disguising the want and the pleasure gleaming in her brown eyes. I can't stop kissing her gorgeous mouth, and she's kissing me back with the same hunger, and I will never get enough.

Sex has never felt this good, and I know I'm never going to stop wanting her.

A familiar tingle zips up my spine, and my balls tighten to the point of pain. "Fuck. I need you to come, baby."

"I'm close," she pants as I pivot my hips in deeper.

She groans, rocking her hips up, and I move my fingers down her beautiful body. I pinch her clit hard just as my orgasm hits, and she explodes the same time I do.

I remove the binds from her wrists and pull her into my body, cradling her against me. She curls around me without hesitation, and we wrap our arms around one another, clinging to sweat-slickened skin as we continue to kiss and our hands continue to explore.

I love you.

The words float on my tongue, but I'm too afraid to say it.

Scared she doesn't feel the same.

I know once I go there, there is no going back, and the fear of rejection has me stuffing the words back inside.

"That was amazing, Charlie." She dusts a line of soft kisses along my chest while peering up at me, and I grin at her sex-flushed face and her tangled hair.

"You look thoroughly fucked," I tease, kissing the tip of her nose.

Her eyes glint devilishly as she twists my nipple, and a dart of pleasure-pain ricochets through my body. My cock jerks to life, hardening almost instantly where it nudges against her stomach. She looks at me through hooded eyes, and her lips kick up at the corners. "See, that's where you're wrong." She slides her hand down the gap between our bodies, palming my dick. "I'm nowhere near thoroughly fucked, so quit slacking and get on with the job."

Charlie

I flip her over on her stomach superfast, and she squeals in delight. "Now, you've done it," I whisper, biting her ear. "By the time you leave here, you'll be lucky if you can walk." I yank her butt up in the air, part her legs, and slide home, impaling myself so deep inside her cunt it feels like I'm touching her womb.

Chapter Sixteen
Demi

I glance anxiously at the clock on the wall, wondering if Charlie got delayed at the airport in Arizona because it's not like him to be late. I pull my cell out of my purse again, but there are no new texts. The last one I got was this morning, when he confirmed he was en route to the airport with his mom and sister.

I've never seen Charlie lose his shit quite like he did when he found out Uncle George had a stash of kiddie porn on his home computer and he's a regular visitor to the dark web and a regular viewer of live sex cams where kids are abused by all manner of sickos. I was almost physically ill when Charlie told me, so I understand his reaction.

He had the Barron private jet fueled and ready to depart Logan private airfield in a couple of hours. I wanted to go with him, but he asked me to stay behind, and I didn't argue. I know his relationship with his mom is pretty much nonexistent right now, and he might have a fight on his hands to persuade her to return to Rydeville.

Looks like it was the right call, and I'm relieved they are

both coming back with him. I know how much he's missed his family, and I hope he can repair his relationship with his mother now they will all be living together again.

Of course, that will put an end to the naughty sex sessions we've been having in every room of that house. Since last month, when we finally gave in to our pent-up need for one another, we've been like rabid animals, pouncing on one another the second we're alone.

We're both sticking to the rules at work, but it only heightens our craving for one another outside of the office.

I owe Xena big-time, because she's been going to my house a lot after work to mind Dad while my boyfriend fucks me senseless.

I'm not naïve. I know Charlie is holding back in the bedroom for my sake, and I get an electric thrill every time I think of all the depraved things he plans on doing to my body. He's already pushed me out of my comfort zone, and I'm loving every minute of it.

I've been missing out all these years, because my past lovers didn't reduce my body to a quivering mass in the way Charlie does. His touch does extreme things to me, and I will never get enough of his hands on me.

Fed up of pacing the living room, waiting for my boyfriend, I head into Dad's bedroom to see if he needs anything before I head to the elite ball.

"You look absolutely breathtaking, sweetheart," he says when I enter his room. "I hope Charlie knows how lucky he is."

"Thanks, Dad." I press a kiss to his clammy forehead. He started the experimental trial a couple weeks ago, and the side effects are horrendous. He's barely able to keep anything down, and he's plagued with stomach cramps and continuous headaches. "Can I get you anything before I leave?"

He shuffles up against the headboard, and I hate how his

chest rattles and his breath wheezes out in strangled gasps. He pats the bed beside him. "Come talk to your old man for a minute."

I sit on the edge of the bed, careful not to crease my expensive floor-length gold and green silk gown. I cannot even repeat how much Charlie paid for this. I was aghast when I saw the price tag, but he insisted on paying for it, along with matching shoes and a clutch, and he arranged for Abby and I to have a spa day today where I was pampered and preened to within an inch of my life.

I'm walking on air, living a dream with my very own Prince Charming. Albeit a dark version. I chuckle at my own thought.

Abby has been amazing too. I've been attending her weekly self-defense lessons. She has a private trainer who goes to her house, so I'm a regular at Chez Anderson these days. Charlie usually drives me there, and I know Abby is thrilled that Kai, Drew, and Charlie are mending bridges. We haven't started lessons at the shooting range yet, purely because I don't have the time, but Charlie has offered to sit with Dad on Saturday afternoons so I can go.

"How are you feeling about everything I told you last week?" Dad asks, pulling me out of my thoughts. I hate how feeble his voice sounds. How much he appears to have aged these past few weeks.

Dad finally fessed up to something Charlie has known about. I was a bit peeved Charlie didn't tell me, but he explained it wasn't his secret to tell, and I guess it wasn't.

It turns out that my mom, Luana, met Charlie's dad, Charles, one summer when she was visiting a friend in Rydeville. They fell in love and kept in regular contact after she returned home. They conducted a long-distance romance for a couple of years, and Charles tried to obtain a scholarship for Mom so she could attend Rydeville University with him, but his father intervened. Apparently, Mom wasn't good enough for the son of a founding father, and he deliberately tried to split them up. They kept seeing each other in secret while Mom was a student at UMaine until she bumped into my father one day on campus and they fell hard and fast for one another.

According to Dad, Mom was already preparing to end her relationship with Charles because she had fallen out of love with him. But Charles was heartbroken, and he wanted someone to blame, and Dad was the obvious target.

Mom and Dad were married in less than a year, and six months after they graduated from college, Mom was pregnant with me. Dad's mom, his last surviving parent, passed away a few months before I was born, leaving him the house we now live in. Dad said the decision to move to Rydeville was difficult, but finances were tight, and they had a baby on the way, so they did it even though it meant seeing Charles around.

Dad had been working for an accounting firm a couple of hours' drive away, but once Mom passed, he was forced to resign, because he could no longer commit to the commute as a newly widowed single parent.

Jobs were thin on the ground back then, and he swallowed his pride and approached Charles Barron for work. Charles gave him a job, purely in Mom's memory, and he spent the next twenty-two years ensuring my father was kept firmly under his thumb.

Charlie is shocked and disgusted at how his father treated mine, and I know, from talking to other colleagues at work, that it was unusual for the ex-CEO. From what Charlie has told me, his parents had an epic love, so it seems like Charles drew the longer straw, and he could've been more charitable. Especially when it came to my father's stroke and subsequent paralysis when Charles's treatment of him was particularly cruel.

But the man himself isn't here anymore to explain why he did it or why he was still holding on to a grudge after more than twenty years.

"Demi." Dad nudges me and I realize I've zoned out.

"Sorry. What were you saying?"

"Are you okay with everything I told you last week? About your mom and Charles Barron?"

"It explains a lot." Dad nods. "And I'm glad you got the girl, Dad."

The doorbell chimes, and Mrs. Griffin pops her head in the room a minute later. "Your young man is here, Demi. Looking rather dashing, I might add."

"Thanks, Nora." I kiss Dad's papery cheek. "Love you, Dad."

"Love you too, princess." He smiles. "I wish your mother could be here to see what a wonderful young woman you've become. She'd be so proud of you."

Tears prick my eyes. "She'd be so proud of you too." I clasp his hand, overcome with sudden emotion. "You have showered me with love and support my entire life, made sure I always had everything I needed, and set the best example. I'm the luckiest girl in the world because I have you for my father."

A sob from behind reminds me we're not alone. "You two." Mrs. Griffin sobs, patting her chest. "You get me every time."

"Go have fun, sweetheart," Dad says, shooing me away. "Tell Charlie hi from me."

Charlie is waiting outside on the front path when I emerge. The beam from the porch light bathes him in a golden hue as he slowly turns around, and he literally looks like he dropped down to Earth from heaven.

How did I get so lucky to call him mine?

I suck in a breath as my gaze rakes over his gorgeous body in his sharp, fitted, black tux. His hair is neatly styled back off his face, and his jaw is freshly shaven. "Wow." I smile broadly as I walk toward him. "You look hot."

His eyes seem troubled as they lock on mine.

The smile instantly drops off my face. "What's wrong? Did something happen with your mom and Lil?" Panic bubbles up my throat.

"They're fine," he assures me. His gaze roams over me briefly, and his tormented expression deepens. "You are absolutely breathtaking, Demi. The most beautiful woman I've ever seen."

I melt under his praise, but alarm bells are still ringing in my ears. I step closer, placing my palms on his firm chest. "What's going on, babe?"

Pain flares across his face, and an anxious, fluttering feeling floods my chest cavity. "I'm so sorry, Demi, but I can't do this anymore."

My brows knit together as my hands fall to my sides. "What do you mean? Do what?"

He takes a step back, gesturing between us with his hand. "Us. Relationships. It's not going to work."

"It *is* working," I protest. "I don't understand. What's brought all this on?"

"Today was a potent reminder of the evils of my world. You don't belong in that world, Demi, and I was a fool to think this could work. Thankfully, I've come to my senses before I made things worse."

Pain courses through me, and I'm struggling to breathe. "How can you do this to me?" I close the gap between us. "How can you do this to *us*?" My voice raises as anger blends with my pain. "Things are going great, and I'm prepared for tonight, and—"

A bitter laugh rips from his throat. "You are *not* prepared for tonight," he hisses. "And I was clearly insane to even consider bringing you. They would devour you upon sight."

The implication that I'm weak or naïve or unable to keep my wits about me is the final straw. "Fuck you, Charlie."

He smirks, reminding me that asshole mask he wears is never far from the surface. "Been there, done that, bought the T-shirt." His lips curl into a sneer. "Time to buy a new one."

I slap him across the cheek. "You were right. You don't know how to handle intimacy or relationships. I feel sorry for you, because you will end up bitter and alone."

He shrugs, like my words mean nothing. "See you around, Demi."

Chapter Seventeen
Demi

I crack apart on the inside as I stand rooted to the spot, watching him walk off, like he hasn't a care in the world.

Like he hasn't just irreparably shattered my heart and crushed my soul.

He slips into the back of the blacked-out limousine, and it glides away from the curb a few seconds later.

A sob bursts from my chest, and I hold my hand over my mouth, struggling to hold my emotion at bay. I glance all around, hoping none of the neighbors bore witness to my humiliation. *Couldn't he have decided this before I got all dolled up?* It would've helped minimize the humiliation although nothing could dampen the pain of his rejection.

What to do? I can't go back inside because I don't want to upset Dad. I tap out a text to Xena, and then I tiptoe back into the house, as quiet as a mouse, and retrieve the keys to my Volvo. Then I hop in my car and drive to my bestie's house.

Xena opens the door to me with a bottle of wine in one hand and a carton of Belgian chocolate chip ice cream in the other. "He's a fucking bastard," she says, stepping sideways to let me in.

An errant sob sneaks from my mouth, and my lower lip wobbles as pain presses down on my chest, making breathing difficult. "I love him," I croak, as tears stream down my face. "And he just kicked me aside like I meant nothing to him."

She sets the wine and ice cream down and envelops me in a hug. I fall apart in her arms, clinging to her as the floodgates open and I pour all my anguish out.

"He doesn't deserve you, and he's going to regret ruining the best thing to ever happen to him." She smooths a hand up and down my back as I cry. "Let it all out, babe. Purge the devil from your soul."

I half-laugh through my tears, but nothing can heal the cracks appearing all over my heart.

I sob into her shoulder, dampening her shirt, and she whispers comforting words as she holds me. We hug it out for a while until my tears finally dry. "I'm okay now." I ease out of her embrace, sniffing.

"You're going to be fine," she reassures me, pulling two wine glasses out of a cupboard.

"Where are the guys?" I inquire, anxiously looking around.

"Bo is working, and Leo is at a friend's bachelor party. We have the place to ourselves."

"Can I borrow something to wear?" I desperately need to get out of this dress.

"Of course. Help yourself. You know where my closet is."

Clothing options are limited because we're not the same size, but I find a pair of sweats and a loose-fitting shirt that works, and I pad out to the living room in my bare feet.

"You look beautiful, by the way," she says, handing me the ice cream and a spoon as I join her on the couch.

"He had the nerve to tell me that too." I savagely attack the ice cream carton.

"I don't understand it. Those times we hung out, he seemed devoted to you."

"He thinks he's protecting me," I admit, slurping ice cream from the spoon, the taste barely registering over the taste of my anger.

I've thought about it on the drive over, and it's the only explanation that makes sense. I haven't told her the stuff Charlie told me about the elite because he told me that in confidence, and I think even knowing is risky, so she's in the dark. "But he's taken the coward's way out. He might as well have just called me weak to my face, because that's really what he means. He doesn't think I'm tough enough for his world." I stab the spoon into the tub again, imagining it's Charlie's face.

"It's his loss, babe. And I bet he realizes that soon and regrets it."

***

Abby shows up at my house on Sunday, seething over the way Charlie has treated me. She blew up my cell last night with concerned texts, and I'm touched she cares enough to check in with me in person. "He's an idiot, but his heart is in the right place. He's just scared something will happen to you and that's clouded his judgement."

"What's done is done, Abby. He dumped me cruelly, leaving me standing at my front door like poor Cinderella. If he cared for me at all, he wouldn't have done that."

"Don't give up on him," she pleads, taking my hands in hers. "He's been so happy with you. He'll come around."

"I'm not sure I want him to. He clearly has no faith in me."

She vehemently shakes her head. "It's not that at all.

Mixing in elite circles is dangerous, and he's been worried sick this past month about exposing you to those bastards. I thought I'd convinced him, but I obviously hadn't."

"Wait." I pin her with a suspicious look. "Are you saying he's been having doubts all along?"

"Not about you. He loves you."

I snort. "He doesn't love me."

Her features soften. "He hasn't told you?"

"Nope." I cross my arms over my chest. "And it doesn't matter now."

"He loves you. I'm sure of it. He's probably just afraid to tell you, but he's crazy about you. He wouldn't have done this otherwise. I told him you were strong enough to face the elite shit, and that I'd help, but the memory of what happened to me is too fresh in his mind, and he couldn't take that risk. He's done this because he loves you so much he wants to shield you from them."

"What exactly happened to you? Charlie never elaborated."

"Bad shit I don't like thinking about let alone discussing," she says, averting her eyes.

"I'm sorry for whatever you went through."

She squeezes my hand. "Thank you. I survived it, and arguably, I'm stronger for it. The thing about these guys is they think we're too fragile to think for ourselves." She rolls her eyes. "They think we can't properly protect ourselves. I've been fighting that misconception for as long as I can remember. It's complete bullshit, but they think they need to be these tough, alpha assholes, to keep their women safe."

A ghost of a smile appears on my face.

"Charlie will wise up and realize the safest place for you is in his arms. He'll see you for the strong, independent woman you are. And he'll feel like the biggest piece of shit for letting you go."

"I know you mean well, Abby, and I'm so grateful you dropped by, but Charlie and I are finished. I don't care if he crawls back to me on his hands and knees. All he had to do was talk to me about his concerns so we could discuss it like two grown-ups, but instead he made the decision for me. I can't be in a relationship with a guy like that, and the best thing he can do for me is to act like I don't exist."

On Monday, when I show up for work to find my desk moved to the finance department, I wonder if Abby relayed my request to Charlie and he waved his magic wand and made it happen. I guess I should be pleased I've been promoted, but it feels more like a demotion to me despite the pay increase and new duties.

The pointed fingers and whispers behind my back don't help. Nor does the smug grin on Corrinna Smith's face as she gleefully goes through the details of my new contract with me. She could easily have one of her minions do this, but I'm guessing she wants to wallow in my misery like everyone else.

I've seen the way she flirts with him.

She probably thinks she has a chance with him now. Perhaps, she does. He's probably already returned to his man slut ways.

A fresh wave of pain settles on my chest at that thought. I spent a sleepless night on Saturday wondering if Charlie had taken some elite beauty to his bed. But no good comes from thinking about that shit, so I lock Charlie away in a sealed box, determined to leave him in the past.

The next month is pure hell, and if I thought time would heal my broken heart, I was sorely mistaken.

No breakup has ever affected me like this.

No guy has ever stubbornly lingered in my thoughts like this.

No pain has ever gutted me, night after night, quite like this.

It feels like I'll never recover.

Like I'm destined to live the rest of my life with this constant ache in my chest.

He avoids me like the plague at work and at Abby's house, and it hurts.

I hate that I miss him.

But I miss him so much.

And it's not getting any easier.

I'm standing at the copier on Thursday at lunchtime when I overhear a conversation I wish I hadn't. Two interns are gossiping at a desk behind me, knowing full and well I'm in earshot. "I hear Charlie Barron has moved on with Corrinna Smith," one of them says.

"I heard that too," the second bitch concurs. "Apparently, he's taking her as his date to that management dinner tonight."

"They make such a gorgeous couple," the first bitch says. "Imagine how adorable their kids would be."

I slam the top of the photocopier down, grabbing my documents, and shooting them a scathing look as I return to my desk. This wouldn't be the first time I've had to endure such shit, and I'm officially done.

I retrieve my resume from my personal folder in the cloud and begin updating it. Then I scroll through some recruitment websites, and apply for a few jobs, uncaring if anyone sees what I'm doing.

At this point, getting the hell out of his building is all I care about. I cannot stay here and watch Charlie parade that gold digger on his arm. I've got more pride than that.

It feels like the rest of the day drags, and when five o'clock finally rolls around, I'm the first up out of my chair for a change. I head down in the elevator, needing to put as much distance between me and this place as I can.

My heels make a clacking sound as I dash across the lobby. I'm torturing myself with images of Charlie and Corrinna, so I'm not paying attention, and I almost slam into Charlie and Simon Reed as they shake hands just in front of the entrance doors.

"Demi!" Simon's eyes light up. "I was disappointed to hear you had moved although congratulations on your promotion." His smile is appreciative as he casts a quick glance over me.

All the tiny hairs are standing at attention on the nape of my neck, and I can feel Charlie embedding daggers in my spine as I give him my back, purposely avoiding looking at him or even acknowledging him.

As far as I'm concerned, he's dead to me now.

"Thank you." I smile sweetly at Simon, batting my eyelashes in a deliberate attempt to flirt.

I'm in the mood to inflict some pain.

Although, Charlie probably won't give a flying fuck, considering he's already moved on.

"I'm disappointed we didn't get an opportunity to work together on the project," I tell Simon, "but I'm delighted you won the business. I guess congratulations are in order for you too."

"We should celebrate."

"That sounds like a plan."

Behind me, Charlie's energy field is like a thunderstorm hovering overhead, ready to wreak havoc across the sky at any moment.

"How about dinner? Tomorrow night after work?" he asks.

Simon is attractive, smart, and easy to talk to. But there is zero chemistry between us. Ordinarily, I would shut him down because I can tell from the hope in his eyes that he doesn't feel the same, and I don't like leading guys on. But I'm still so freaking pissed, and quite frankly, a night of good food and good conversation is just what the doctor ordered. "That sounds wonderful."

"Demi has to work overtime tomorrow," Charlie barks, injecting himself into the conversation.

"No, I don't." I still refuse to look at him, so he moves around me, standing beside Simon so I have no choice but to see him and his disgustingly perfect face.

"Your boss obviously hasn't spoken to you yet, but you're not available tomorrow night."

The air is knocked out of my lungs as we stare at one another for the first time in weeks. Pain obliterates every part of me, and my legs feel like they might go out from under me. Tension bleeds into the air, and I know I need to reply to his statement, to call him out on his bullshit, but I'm too heartsore to do it.

"Ah, I see." Simon's smile is flat. "I didn't realize there was something going on between you two."

"There isn't," I say the same time Charlie says, "There is."

Simon takes a step back. "I wish you well, Ms. Alexander." He tips his head at Charlie. "I will see you at the meeting on Monday."

"Thank you, Simon. I'll see you then," Charlie grits out, and I can tell it's killing him to act polite.

I grab the strap of my bag and force my limbs to move. But I've only taken two steps away when Charlie takes hold of my elbow. "Don't go."

"Take your hand off me."

He moves in front of me before dropping his hold. "Can we talk?"

I fold my arms across my chest. "No. I have nothing to say to you."

"Well, I have plenty to say to you."

"I don't care." I glare at him, ignoring the voice squealing in my ear to hear him out. I stomp off, but he follows me.

"I made a mistake, Demi. I was stupid, and I can't live without you. I want you back. I—"

I whirl around, anger blazing in my eyes. "You are too fucking late, Charlie. I don't want to hear your pathetic excuses. You tossed me away without even talking about your concerns, and you think I'll waltz back into your arms because you've realized you were a complete fucktard and you've decided you want me back?"

I'm aware I'm talking way too loud, and that people are listening, but I have zero fucks to give anymore. "That is not how this works." I shove at his chest. "Stay the hell away from me. As far as I'm concerned, you are dead to me. Go cozy up to your new redheaded girlfriend instead. Maybe, she'll buy your bullshit because I'm not."

I storm out of the building, wishing today hadn't been the day my Volvo decided not to start. Because it's lashing rain outside, and I'm quaking all over as the aftermath of the adrenaline rush leaves me unsteady on my feet. I walk in the pouring rain to the bus stop, ruing the day I ever stepped foot in that building, wishing I had never laid eyes on Charlie Barron.

I climb on the bus, soaked to my skin with hair plastered to my face, and I wish I could snap my fingers and be at home in my jammies, snuggled up with Dad in front of the fire, watching one of his historical documentaries.

I'm halfway home when my cell pings. I pick up, and I'm instantly alarmed as Mrs. Griffin's sobs trickle down the line.

"What's happened? Is Dad okay?"

"I'm so sorry, sweetie. Your dad collapsed. He's having trouble breathing. I called an ambulance, and they'll be here any minute."

The world blurs, my stomach churns, and I clutch the handrail in front of me, gripping the metal as tight as I can, needing something to ground me in time and place because I'm floundering. A silent scream builds and builds inside me, and I hop up, pressing the bell, pushing past people in my haste to get to the top. I drop my cell, and Mrs. Griffin's voice can be heard calling me. I pick it up with trembling fingers as the driver stops the bus and I get out. I press my cell to my ear, and my voice is as hollow as my heart as I speak. "I'll meet you at the hospital."

I pull the Uber app up on my cell and book a car to take me there.

Then, I sit down on a bench and pray like I've never prayed before.

Chapter Eighteen
Charlie

I purposely sit in a different seat when I return to the table after visiting the bathroom, because I have officially reached the limits of my patience reserves and I cannot bear another second in Corrinna Smith's company.

For an educated woman, she sure is dumb as fuck, continuing to paw at me and blatantly flirt when I have made it clear, over and over, that I am not interested nor will I ever be interested.

I make a mental note to ask Arthur if there is protocol in place for firing the chief human relations officer because I want that poisonous bitch gone from my business.

After Demi's cryptic comment earlier, I went straight to Margaret Ann to get the lowdown.

Margaret is the ultimate professional, and she's not one to spread gossip, but she has her ear to the ground in the office, and if I ever need to know something, I always go to her. It helps that she's known me since I was a little boy and she trusts me.

Demi mentioned a redhead, and it didn't take much to

connect the dots. I asked Margaret point-blank if there was gossip about me and Corrinna and she spewed without hesitation.

That gold-digging bitch spread the word around the office that she was my date tonight, knowing it would get back to Demi and sabotage any chances of us reuniting.

It's my fault because when she suggested I bring her as my official date, earlier in the week, I told her the only woman I would consider bringing anywhere as my date was Demi because she was the love of my life and I was going to try to patch things up with her.

I thought she would take the hint and take a hike, but I should've known she would turn nasty.

Now, everything I planned is ruined because Demi won't even give me the time of day let alone allow me to whisk her away for the weekend.

I know I fucked up big-time.

That I needed to make a grand gesture to try to make up for it.

And I instantly knew what I wanted to do. Because Demi is *the one*. There is zero hesitation in my mind, and I need her to see I'm serious about our future and that I won't ever push her away again.

I've spent all week putting plans in place. Groveling to her dad and her best friend. Laying my heart on the line as I begged them to help me, finally winning their support when I showed them the pretty gold-colored diamond engagement ring I've bought her and told them of my plans to whisk her away to Cape Neddick by private jet and propose to her on Nubble Light, Maine's most famous lighthouse, which also happens to be the very place where her parents got engaged.

Henry mentioned that during one of our talks, and I filed it away for future reference. I've booked a gorgeous property, close to the lighthouse, for the entire weekend because I want to make our engagement a memory to cherish forever.

But that's shot to hell now, thanks to that spiteful bitch.

My phone pings in my pocket, and I pull it out, ignoring the fake hurt looks Corrinna is throwing my way from across the table. I have no doubt she'll be over here as soon as she can extricate herself from her current conversation, but I'm not planning on sticking around.

These management events bore the shit out of me, and I've got more urgent places I need to be. If I could've gotten out of it, I would've been groveling at Demi's door hours ago, but I couldn't, so I swore I would stay until dinner was over and then make my excuses.

I frown as I spot the numerous missed calls from Abby, Drew, and Kai. I'd turned my phone off while we were having dinner, and now, I'm sorry I did, because something is clearly wrong.

Fear causes goose bumps to sprout on my arms as I accept Abby's call now, jumping up, narrowly avoiding bumping into the waitress distributing dessert to the table. "What's wrong?" I ask before she can speak.

"I'm at the hospital. It's Demi's dad. He's had a heart attack, and it's not looking good."

"I'm on my way." I hang up, hustling toward where Arthur sits. "I've got to go."

"Is everything okay?"

"Henry Alexander is in the hospital. Demi needs me."

"Go. And keep me updated."

I feel Corinna's eyes on me as I race out of the restaurant.

I pace the sidewalk as I wait for my driver to emerge from the underground parking lot.

I sit with my face in my hands in the back seat of my car, praying I get there in time.

I bump into people as I run through the hospital doors, pushing my way into the elevator, ignoring the filthy looks, because all I care about is being there for Demi.

Kai is in the corridor when I emerge from the elevator. "Any news?" I ask.

"All we know is he's had a coronary and he's in surgery now."

"How is she?"

"Barely holding it together."

"Take me to her."

"This way," Kai says, lifting one shoulder. "I don't know how she'll react to your presence, but it's good you're here."

"I wouldn't want to be anywhere else." We stop outside the door to the waiting room. I clamp my hand on his shoulder. "I just want to say thanks. I think I'd still have my head stuck up my ass if it wasn't for our conversation."

"I know you would have." He smirks, punching me in the upper arm. "Like I said, I totally understand. I tried to shield Abby from it too until I realized she was safest with me. You know how the elite work. It doesn't matter that you pushed Demi away to protect her. They could find out about her in a heartbeat and still use her against you. The safest way of ensuring she's safe is keeping her close."

"The thought of anything happening to her kills me, Kai. I would burn the world down if anyone hurt her. Mom and Lil too."

I'm so glad my family is back home where they belong. Where I can keep an eye on them and keep them safe. Mom and I still have some way to go, but when she told me she's forgiven me, I broke down and sobbed like a baby. I know it's going to be all right, and now, I just need to win back the girl I love.

Demi is the only girl who matters.

She's the only girl I want for now and always.

"We won't let anything happen to them," he reassures me, and I'm glad I let my stubborn pride go and mended shit with my friends, because with the stuff coming down the line, we need to stick together as a united team.

The elite ball was a real eye-opener. The new president said all the right things, but everything we suspected is coming to fruition. The reorganizing committee is just a PR exercise to make it look like he's committed to change when he's most definitely not.

We've all been summoned to the newly constructed Parkhurst—now housed in some sprawling private facility in Virginia—for some final initiation tasks in two months. Abby and Vanessa have been summoned too, which is cause for concern, along with Harley and Joaquin. The mothers haven't been included, but we've no doubt plans are afoot there too.

So, yeah, shit is getting real. And I need to ensure my loved ones are safe before it all kicks off.

"You ready, man?" Kai asks, curling his hand around the door handle.

"As I ever will be."

We step into the small waiting room, mostly occupied with people here for Henry. Xena is here with her boyfriends. Drew is chatting quietly with Shandra while Olivia and Sylvia are talking with Margaret Ann.

Abby jumps up when she sees me. "I'm glad you're here," she whispers. "She's distraught."

"I can see that," I say, my eyes glued to Demi's trembling shoulders. She's seated in the far corner with Mrs. Griffin. Demi is hunched over with her head in her hands, her dark hair falling around her face like a curtain. Mrs. Griffin has her arm wrapped tight around her shoulders, whispering words of comfort, no doubt.

"I know you had big plans this weekend, Charlie, but she doesn't need to hear any of that right now."

I gawk at her. "I am not a complete imbecile."

"Could've fooled me," Xavier says, entering the room from behind, carrying a tray with coffees. Hunt slips in behind him with another tray, and they start distributing them.

"Rick is in the air," Kai says, hauling Abby into his arms. "Hopefully, he can talk to some of the doctors and find out what's going on."

I take a coffee from Hunt, nodding gratefully, as I extricate myself from the conversation and walk to Demi.

Mrs. Griffin lifts her head up, smiling softly when she sees me. She knows about my plans because I've already paid her handsomely to stay with Henry this weekend.

"I'm going to take a little trip to the bathroom," she says, giving Demi's shoulders one last squeeze.

I sit down on Demi's other side as she lifts her head. She watches Mrs. Griffin walk off before she slowly turns to face me. Her eyes are bloodshot and swollen, her face puffy and red from crying. "Hey." I hand her the coffee, and she curls her fingers around it while staring straight through me. "How are you holding up?"

She stares numbly at me. "Why are you here?" she asks, her voice devoid of emotion.

"I came the instant I found out because I want to be here for you."

"Why?" She hugs the coffee cup to her chest.

I smother my nerves because this isn't about me. "Because I love you. And I love your dad. And there is nowhere else I want to be but right here holding your hand and cradling you in my arms, reminding you that you are not alone, because you have me. You have always had me."

Her lower lips wobbles, and silent tears roll down her face.

Gently, I pry the cup from her hands and set it aside. I open my arms. "Come here."

I expect her to hesitate or to refuse, but she falls against me, collapsing in a river of tears.

Quietly, our friends exit the room, giving us some privacy. In the other corner, a young child is asleep in his father's lap. The man nods, and I smile at him as I wrap my arms tighter around Demi.

"I'm so scared, Charlie." She sniffles, clutching my shirt as she sobs into my chest.

"I know, baby." I press a kiss to her hair. "We just have to pray he comes through this."

She looks at me through blurry eyes. "I don't want him to die," she sobs, "but I feel so selfish for thinking that since he has little quality of life."

"I heard the treatment wasn't working, and I've seen how weak he's become."

"What? How?" Her tears dry up.

"I've been visiting him every week. I made him promise not to tell you."

"Why?"

"Because I care about him, and I wanted to know if the treatment was working." I brush hair back off her face. "I was sorry to hear it wasn't."

"I can't believe he didn't tell me. We tell each other everything."

I clear my throat. "I wanted him to understand why I pushed you away. I've been talking to him about the elite. Sharing my concerns and fears. Letting him know I love you with my whole heart but I'm terrified about dragging you into this world. And he's been talking to me, helping me work things out, speaking about your mom, and my dad, and I guess we've been getting to know each other a bit better."

It was a combination of Kai's and Henry's advice that convinced me to fight for love. Knowing Demi's dad supports me was a game changer. I laid it all on the line. He's worried about her, there's no doubt about that, but he believes in my ability to protect her and keep her safe, and he told me he could die in peace knowing his little girl was going to be looked after.

"What about Corrinna?" she asks, swiping at the moisture under her eyes.

"She lied in a deliberate attempt to thwart my plans. I stupidly told her I was planning on winning you back." I kiss the end of her nose. "I'm sorry if that hurt you but I can assure you I have zero interest in that woman. The only woman I care about, the only woman I love, is you."

She flings her arms around my neck, hugging me tight. "I love you too," she whispers. "I love you so much, and I've been in so much pain."

"I know, baby." I dot kisses all over her face. "It's killed me too. Can you ever forgive me?"

"I already have," she says, her eyes welling up again.

I blink a few times, amazed at her generosity and her ability to forgive so easily. "I don't deserve that, but thank you."

"I was so mad earlier," she says. "And I meant every word of what I said, but these past few hours I've been sitting here, thinking about how unpredictable life is, how short our time is with our loved ones, and I don't want to waste precious time arguing with you." She palms my cheek. "We still have stuff to discuss, and you are going to grovel." She pins me with a stern expression. "But all that matters is, we love each other."

"And we can't live without one another," I add, rubbing my nose against hers.

"And we're in this together no matter what the future holds," she says.

"Together," I agree.

Charlie

Her smile is sad, but as we hold one another, I know we will get through the tough times, because I will hold her up at times when she needs it, and she will be my strength when I need to lean on her.

I hold her flush to my body as I press my lips to her mouth, pouring all my love into my kiss, letting her feel my commitment and my determination, so she knows, without a shadow of doubt, that she will never shoulder any burden alone again.

Chapter Nineteen
Demi

"I got you some more stuff from your house," Charlie says, entering Dad's private room in the hospital and dropping a duffel bag on the tile floor at my feet.

"Thank you." I rub his arm as he leans down, pressing a soft kiss to my lips.

"Any change?" he asks, sinking into the seat beside me and wrapping his arm around my shoulders.

I shake my head, unable to form the words. These past four days have been extremely difficult, and I doubt I'd be holding it together if it weren't for Charlie. He's my rock, and I'm glad he's here. He only leaves to grab food or pick up more clothes for me from my house, and I know he'd sleep here too if the nurses didn't throw him out every night and if he didn't have a family at home waiting for him. Charlie's only just reconnected with his mom and sister, and I don't want to come between them—no matter how often he tells me they understand.

"Has the doctor been around yet?" He holds me tight, planting a kiss in my hair.

"He should be here any minute now." I've come to dread

the daily doctor's visits because the news is never good. Dad had a massive heart attack, depriving his brain of oxygen, and he's been in a coma ever since. Deep down, I know what it means, but I can't face it. Not until I'm forced to. I squeeze Dad's hand, needing the comfort of his warm skin against mine even though I know it's only an illusion. Dad's body is failing, and there's no coming back from this. "And I think today's the day." Where he tells me there's no point keeping him on life support any longer.

"I'm here, babe. Whatever he says, we'll face it together." He kisses my cheek, and his eyes shine with compassion. "I might have to step out for a little while this afternoon to take a con call," he adds. We've both taken time off work, but Charlie is the president, so he still needs to take calls and check emails, and he works on and off from this room with an iPad in his lap. "I couldn't get out of it, but otherwise, I'm stuck to your side."

"I appreciate everything you've done." I gently cup his face. "I can only do this because you're with me."

He kisses the tip of my nose. "You don't give yourself enough credit, babe. You are one of the strongest people I know. But I'm glad I'm here with you, and I'm going nowhere."

I snuggle in to him, glad we've reconciled, because I don't want to live another day without him by my side.

The door creaks as it opens, and I turn stiff in Charlie's arms. I glance over my shoulder as blood rushes to my head, making me dizzy. My heart thumps behind my rib cage and bile pools at the base of my throat as I take one look at the doctor's face. A whimper escapes my lips, and tears instantly spring forth.

"Ms. Alexander." The doctor shoots me a sympathetic look as he takes the vacant seat on the other side of Dad's bed. "I'm sorry to be the bearer of bad news, but I think you know this has been coming."

Tears stream down my face as I nod.

"Our latest tests show minimal brain activity and acute organ failure. It's time." He stands, smiling sadly at Dad. "Take as long as you need to say your goodbyes." He rounds the bed, planting a soft hand on my shoulder. "I'm very sorry, Demi."

Charlie bundles me in his arms as tears flow freely down my face. Intense pressure settles on my chest, and I'm swallowing painfully over the anguished lump clogging my throat. I cling to Charlie as the dam breaks and everything I've been holding inside explodes. My tormented cries bounce off the pale blue walls as I fall apart. Charlie holds me through it all, whispering endearments and reassurances, bolstering me with his strong arms, a slew of promises, his warmth, and his vitality.

Eventually, I stop—when my throat is raw, my eyes are stinging, and my heart feels like a hollow block of stone in my chest.

"Do you want me to call anyone?" Charlie quietly inquires.

"Xena and Mrs. Griffin. I think they'd like to say goodbye."

I drape my arms around Dad's chest as I listen to Charlie make the calls.

"I have sent a car to pick them up," he confirms a few minutes later. "Do you want me to leave so you can say goodbye in private?"

I reach around for his hand, clasping it tight, as I shake my head. "I want you here."

He rubs soothing circles on the back of my hand as I face my father. "Daddy," I choke out, barely able to speak over the lump blocking my throat. My eyes burn and my vision blurs as more tears form. "Thank you for giving me life and for showing me what it means to be a compassionate, caring person. Thank you for loving me like you did. For sacrificing so much to ensure I'm the person I am today. I have so many wonderful memories that I will cherish from now until the day I die. I couldn't have asked for a better father, and while I hate that our time together has been cut short, I love that you are about to be reunited with Mom."

Tears leak out of my eyes as I hang my head and sob. Charlie envelops me in his arms, from behind, offering strong, silent support. "I don't want you to worry about me, because I'm going to be okay, so you can let go now, Dad." I straighten up, and Charlie loosens his hold. I bend down, kissing Dad on the forehead. "I love you, Daddy. For now and always. Go find Mom. Be at peace." I kiss his leathery cheek, noting how he no longer smells like himself. This shell of a body is just that. Dad's spirit is already floating above this world.

Xena and Mrs. Griffin arrive, and there are more tearful goodbyes. Charlie is stoic through it all. Holding me up. Letting me know he's in this for the long haul. When the time comes to switch off the machine, I hold Xena's hand in one hand and Mrs. Griffin's hand in my other while Charlie hugs me at the waist from behind. We stand, united as one, watching my father pass from this life to the next, and it's surreal that I'll never see him again.

He'll never be waiting with a smile and a warm plate of dinner when I arrive through the door in the evening. He won't ever be huddled in front of the TV, immersed in one of the documentaries he so loved, his eyes alight with excitement while he pats the empty space beside him, eager for me to sit so he can fill me in. He won't ever again greet me with open arms, ready to offer me comfort when I've had a bad day.

The man who tucked me into bed at night, who kissed my grazed knees, soothed my heartache when my schoolgirl crush broke my heart, ferried me to dance classes and basketball practice, fed and clothed and educated me, is gone, and he exists now only in my memories. I vow to always keep them alive, to never forget everything we shared, and to never forget the man he was, because he truly was one in a million and I'm blessed to have called him my dad.

Charlie attends to the paperwork while I console a sobbing Mrs. Griffin. Then, we exit the hospital together. Our parting is hazy, because I'm merely going through the motions, as if I'm drifting above the world. I'm vaguely aware of hugging them goodbye, of Charlie ushering me into the back seat of his chauffeur-driven Merc, of resting my head against his shoulder while I lean on him for support.

We pull up in front of his house some time later. "Demi." His warm hands clasp my cheeks. "I want you to stay here tonight, but if you'd prefer to go home, I can grab a bag and come with."

I stare at him forlornly. "I don't know if I can face my house." Not knowing all Dad's things are still there. That his scent lingers. And memories fill every room. My heart is too fragile to cope right now.

"Let's go inside. Get something to eat and get you settled. If you change your mind, we can leave any time."

I nod, letting him help me out of the car. His driver removes my bag from the trunk and hands it to Charlie.

The front door opens, and I attempt to smile at the beautiful dark-haired woman filling the doorway, but it's an effort because I'm numb inside.

"Mom, this is Demi," Charlie says, keeping his arm around my shoulders as we reach the door.

"Come into the warmth," Mrs. Barron says, stepping aside to let us enter.

The instant the door is closed, she hauls me into her arms, hugging me close. "I'm so sorry for your loss, honey, and I wish we were meeting under different circumstances."

I can only nod.

"I made soup and sandwiches," she says. "I know you probably don't feel like eating, but you should try." She eases me out of her embrace, taking my hand in hers. "Why don't you put Demi's bag upstairs and meet us in the kitchen," she says to Charlie.

"Sure." He kisses the top of my head. "I'll be right back."

Mrs. Barron leads me into the kitchen, holding out a chair for me at the table. I sit down as if on autopilot. She places a steaming bowl of vegetable soup in front of me a couple minutes later and a large plateful of sandwiches in the center of the table. She takes the chair beside me, her hands wrapping around a coffee cup. "I understand what you are going through, Demi, and I just want you to know that we are all here for you." She wipes a tear from my cheek. "My son loves you dearly, and I know Lillian and I are going to love you dearly too." She puts her coffee down, and a look of fierce determination sweeps over her face. "There is no handbook on grief, and it hits every person differently." She pats my hand. "So, you take whatever time you need." She brushes my hair behind my ears. "And you are welcome to stay here for as long as you want. Let us take care of you. Let Charlie take care of you because that boy has the biggest heart."

I smile through my tears. "I've seen that," I whisper. "And he's already taking such good care of me."

"Because I love you," Charlie says, walking into the room and overhearing our conversation. "And I'm always going to look after you."

In the days ahead, Charlie more than proves his words. He attends the funeral home with me, helping to confirm arrangements. And on the day of the funeral, he never leaves my side. At night, he holds me close as I cry a river, encouraging me to let it all out, never once asking for anything for himself.

Days turn to weeks, and life slowly goes on. I return to the office to discover Corrinna Smith has been fired. Charlie asks if

I want my old role back, but I decline. Now that we are officially a couple, I think it's best we work in separate divisions within the company.

A month after Dad's death, I feel strong enough to return to the house. Charlie has gradually moved all my things over to his place, but I still need to go through Dad's stuff. Charlie, Abby, Drew, and Kai help me pack up the house, and it's cathartic even though it's heartbreaking.

I'm not sure what to do with the house.

All I know is I don't want to sell it yet. It's been in my family for over a hundred years, and it's the house where I grew up and Dad grew up, so I'm not ready to part with it. Maybe, I never will be. All I know for sure is I can't live there now. The ghosts of the past are too prevalent, and I can't bear to live there without Dad.

So, I settle into Charlie's house. Sharing his bedroom and his life. Getting to know Elizabeth and Lillian and forming bonds with my new family.

It's the fresh start I so desperately need, and, as the weeks turn to months, gradually the constant ache in my chest becomes less intense.

Epilogue
Charlie

Tears glisten in Demi's eyes, but this time, they're happy tears. "Yes, you beautiful, complicated man. Yes, I'll marry you."

Thank fuck. I climb to my feet, slide the engagement ring on her finger, and kiss the shit out of her, and then, I sweep her in to my arms, swinging her around as warmth invades every part of me. Demi's presence in my life has banished the cold, empty feeling that used to reside inside me, infusing me with warmth and light and more joy than I thought I'd ever experience.

She lights up my life in so many ways, and I never believed love could be like this. She is my whole world, and I can't ever imagine living without her.

She laughs, and the sound does funny things to my insides. Demi was a shell of herself for months as she struggled with grief. I've had recent experience with it too, so I knew to let her process it in her own time, and I just tried to be here for her, in whatever capacity she needed.

Mom has been amazing with her, and they have bonded in

a way I only dreamed of. Mom is still grieving too, but having Demi around has been good for both of them. And Lil loves her to bits. They hang out a lot, go shopping, and have spa days, and I know Lil's confiding in Demi about boys and shit I really don't want to know. It's as if she's always lived here, and she's helping fill the gap left by Dad's larger-than-life presence.

Uncle George was put away for a few years, and I feel good that I had Xavier send a file anonymously to the police. That is one less monster walking the streets preying on innocent kids.

But the elite threat is all too real, and now, I'm a full member of Parkhurst, along with my friends, we fully intend on doing something about it. It's clear President Hamilton wants to keep us close so he can control us, but he underestimates our determination. None of us will rest easy until they've all been taken down. For now, protecting Demi and keeping her and my family safe is my sole priority.

"You make me so happy," she murmurs, drawing me out of my mind. I banish all thoughts of elite shit as I place her feet on the ground, focusing on the beautiful woman circling her arms around my neck.

"You make me happy too, babe." I rub my nose against hers. "Especially when you're naked and spread wide open on my bed." I waggle my brows as blood rushes to my cock, swelling it instantly. It's just as well I moved my bedroom over to the other side of the house, far from innocent ears, because we've used the last six months to get better acquainted under the sheets.

Demi has readily handed over responsibility for her sexual satisfaction to me, and I've enjoyed pushing her out of her comfort zone as we explore new desires. I think she's happy to lose herself in me every night because it's a distraction from her grief, and I've loved showering her with pleasure and reminding her that life is still very much for living.

No matter how often I have her, whether it's rough sex or

intimate lovemaking, I am never sated because I cannot get enough of this woman. Every experience is a new experience, and I crave her body in a way I've never known.

She playfully swats at my chest. "We're not wasting that gorgeous dinner, and I want a PG-rated memory I can share with our future children."

I grab her ass cheeks, pulling her pussy tight against my hard-on. "We can eat dinner, and I'll give you that romantic proposal story for our kids and grandkids, but I'm having *you* for dessert." I nip at her earlobe, and she shrieks.

"Damn you, Charlie." She smacks my ass. "Now, I'll be squirming eating dinner."

We grab a couple of selfies before reluctantly leaving the lighthouse. They don't usually allow visitors into the actual lighthouse, but, like most things in life, flashing the cash worked, and they granted me permission to propose to my girl here.

"Did my dad tell you he proposed to my mom here?" Demi asks as we stroll hand in hand toward the parking lot.

"He did." I glance at her, hoping this won't upset her. "I was going to propose to you six months ago, and your dad helped me plan it."

She slams to a halt, pressing a hand to her chest as tears well in her eyes. "He knew?" she whispers.

I nod, placing my hands on her hips. "I asked him for your hand in marriage, and he gave us his blessing. I was looking for someplace special to propose, and he told me how he proposed to your mom here, and I knew this was the place." I pull her into my arms and turn us so we're facing the lighthouse. "I think we'll have to make it a formal family tradition. One we pass on to our children. What do you think?"

"I think I love you so much my heart is fit to burst."

"Ditto, Mrs. Barron." I press my mouth to hers. Our kiss is

slow and sensual, and a deep sense of contentment fills me as her love wraps around me.

"I'm not Mrs. Barron yet," Demi rasps when we finally tear our mouths apart.

"I'm hoping you will be soon," I admit, linking our fingers together. "I'd like a short engagement because I can't wait to officially call you mine."

"There's no need to wait," she agrees. "I'm dying to marry you."

I kiss her more passionately this time, rocking my hips against hers so she feels what she does to me.

"We'd better leave before I throw caution to the wind and let you take me here," she murmurs against my lips.

"Are you trying to kill me?" I joke, adjusting myself in my pants.

"You do the same to me, you know," she says, taking my hand and leading us along the path. "You just can't see it on the outside."

That does it. I push her against the railing and drop to my knees for the second time tonight. My hands glide up her legs, inching up under her knee-length dress.

"Oh my God. You're crazy," she pants. "I thought I was dessert."

"I've changed my mind," I say, my fingers brushing against her lace-clad pussy. "You're the appetizer." I push her thong aside, plunging two fingers into her slick warmth. "You're as horny as me."

"You say that like it's a surprise," she says, spreading her legs wide and granting me full access.

"I don't take anything about us for granted, babe." I pump my fingers in and out of her, reveling in the flush staining her cheeks and the way she bites down on her lower lip.

"Charlie, you turn me on so much. I will never get enough."

I yank her panties down her legs, part her folds with my thumbs, and dive in to my own personal heaven. I lick and suck her just how she likes it, using my fingers and my tongue to bring her to the brink of ecstasy. It's dark out, and the center is closed, but I still keep a lookout, ensuring no one is watching us. When I'm sure it's safe, I wrap my lips around her tight bundle of nerves and suck hard as my fingers thrust faster inside her. She comes with a scream, clutching onto my shoulders as her legs spasm and buckle, and I keep her steady while I extract every last pleasurable wave from her body.

"You are a wicked man," she says as I fix her clothes and stand.

"But you love me."

"I do." She jumps into my arms, and I hold her under her butt as her legs wrap around my waist. "I love you so much." She dusts kisses all over my face as I walk us to the car. "You're my everything, Charlie."

"You are my universe, my love."

Later, after we make it back to the gorgeous house I've rented for the weekend, we eat dinner on the balcony, overlooking the sea, with the sound of crashing waves hitting rocks as a backdrop. We feed one another, constantly touching, and as soon as we've eaten, I lift her in my arms and take her to bed, where we make love all night long.

She stirs in my arms the next morning, and I open my eyes, watching as strips of glorious bright light stream through the open window, bathing her in a golden glow. "Morning, babe." I kiss the corner of her mouth as her eyes blink open.

She moves her hand to my crotch, palming my morning wood. "Morning, sexy." She presses hot kisses to the underside of my prickly jaw before climbing on top of me. Grabbing my erection, she holds it in place as she lowers down on top of me.

I groan as her heat envelops me. "God, you're perfect."

She slides her hands up my chest as she starts rocking slowly on top of me. "Right back at ya. Think of how perfect our kids are going to be."

We stare at one another as we slowly make love, and it still amazes me that I enjoy intimacy this much because I've never known this until Demi. But I'm equally happy when she's tied up on all fours as I slam into her with raw need as I am thrusting inside her slowly, exploring every inch of her soft skin with my hands and my tongue as our eyes connect while we make love.

We come together with the familiarity of two people who know each other's bodies, and wants and desires, inside and out.

She lies on my chest, her dark hair splayed out around us as she draws spirals with her finger on my skin. "How many kids do you want?" she asks, looking up at me.

"At least two, but I'd happily have more if you want."

She props up on one elbow, tracing her fingers along the stubble on my chin and cheeks. "I'd love a big family," she admits. "I always wanted a sibling even though I never told Dad because I didn't want to upset him or make him feel like he had to find a new wife." She looks off into space. "I had a happy childhood, and I've got no real complaints, but it was lonely at times." She locks eyes on me again, smiling. "I love the thought of a bunch of noisy kids filling our house, of a home bursting with laughter and happiness."

I pull her down, kissing her lush mouth, morning breath be damned. "I'm completely sold. When do we get started?"

Epilogue 2

Demi – Ten Years Later

"Jamie! Get down from there," I scream, racing along the beach toward our second-youngest son. He's the daredevil of the bunch and the one most likely to be caught up in mischief. I slow my pace as I watch my husband scale the back of the lifeguard tower after our naughty child, releasing the breath I was holding as soon as Charlie has Jamie safely in his arms.

"He's a handful," Abby says, holding out a chilled bottle of water to me.

"He'll give me gray hairs," I joke, accepting the water gratefully. It's scorching hot today, and I'm jumping up and down continuously, slathering the kids with sunscreen and making sure they're hydrated.

"Kid for sale," Charlie hollers, swinging Jamie around and placing him up on his shoulders.

"Dad wouldn't really sell him, would he?" Jane, our eldest child, and only daughter, asks.

I pull her in close to my side, snaking my arm around her slender shoulders. "Your dad can hardly bear leaving you all at home when he has to go to work every day, so what do you think?"

"He says it a lot," she adds, her brow puckering as she tries to work it out. Jane is only eight, but she carries the weight of the world on her shoulders. I hate that she worries so much, but it's who she is, and I can already tell she's the responsible one in the family, that she will be the one taking care of her brothers and not the other way around.

"He's only joking, doofus," Henry says, landing on the sand in front of us. His dark hair is tousled in messy waves falling over his forehead, and his bright green eyes, so like his father's, twinkle with happiness. "We're building sandcastles, and I need you because Anderson is not winning today."

Abby and I trade an amused expression. "They're more competitive than their dads," she says.

Over the years, any lingering animosity between Charlie and Kai has completely disappeared, and now, they're the best of friends, enjoying boys' nights out and weekend golfing trips in between family time. "I think that's an intrinsic part of the male DNA," I quip. "God help us when they're teenagers." Abby and Kai have four children too, except they have two of each—two sons and two daughters.

Abby groans. "I'm determined to find a way to halt time before that happens."

Henry grabs his sister's arm. "C'mon."

"I wanna build sandcastles," Jamie shrieks, wriggling on top of Charlie's shoulders as they approach.

"You can't come," Henry says. "You only get mad and wreck everything."

"I want to go," Jamie demands, pouting, as Charlie lifts him off his shoulders.

"How about Mom and I take you and baby Charlie for ice

cream?" my husband suggests, knowing full and well that Jamie is a demon for ice cream.

"Go now!" Jamie jumps up and down, clapping his hands.

"One stinky baby coming up," Vanessa says, walking toward me with the offending toddler held at arm's length.

I take my wriggling child from her arms, holding him up and sniffing his diaper-clad butt. "Yup. Someone needs changing." I laugh at the expression on Vanessa's face as Charlie holds his arms out for our youngest. "How did you ever manage when Ren was a baby?" I ask, referring to her six-year-old son with Jackson.

"It's different when it's your own," she says. "And I'm overly sensitive because my senses are all out of whack." She rubs a hand over her swollen belly. "You know how much I love that little cuddle monster," she adds, smiling affectionately at my son. And it's the truth. Since we arrived at the Hamptons a week ago, she has hijacked the baby most days. I think it's fair to say Nessa is dying for the birth of their second child. She had some complications after Ren's birth, and they've had some trouble conceiving, so we were all delighted when they dropped the news of her pregnancy.

"I'll change him," Charlie says, cradling the baby in his arms and nuzzling his chest with his nose. Baby Charlie gurgles, and my husband continues nuzzling him, melting my heart in the process.

"There is just something so incredibly alluring about a man holding a baby," Abby says, and Nessa and I nod. "Every time Kai held one of ours when they were babies, my ovaries about exploded."

"And on that lovely note, we're off," my husband says, leaning in to kiss me. "Handcuff the demon to your side," he jokes, gesturing to where Jamie is attempting to sneak off after his older brother and sister.

"I'm on it." I scoop the little minx up in my arms, dotting kisses all over his face.

"It's a pity the others couldn't make it this time," Nessa says. "It's been ages since we all were on vacation together."

"I know," Abby says, looping my arm through hers as we start walking toward our loungers. "It's getting harder to organize it with work and family life, but I'm glad we could still make it work this year."

"I live for these vacations," I truthfully admit. "Now that I'm at home with the kids all day, I miss adult company. Not that I'm complaining," I add. "Because I'm so grateful I get to stay at home with the kids and be there as they grow up, but I miss working."

"You could help me out if you're interested?" Abby says, as we plow through the hot sand.

Abby runs her own dance studio from a building she leases in Rydeville town square. "In what way?" I ask.

"My accountant just quit. I haven't started looking for a replacement yet. If you're interested, you could work from home or come to the studio and use my office or do a bit of both?"

"That sounds perfect." I hug my cousin and best friend. "We can work out the details when we get home."

"Now, this is what I'm talking about," Jackson says, raising his beer bottle. "To good food, good company, and a kid-free zone for the night."

We all raise our glasses, chinking them together.

"We should get together more often at home," Charlie says, sliding his arm around my shoulders.

"Says the guy who regularly bails because he's got a con call," Kai jokes.

"We can't all be world-famous artists with our own schedule," Charlie replies, grinning.

"I'll have you know my husband works his butt off," Abby says. "And he's got deadlines. His L.A. show is booked for next year, and he's under pressure to finish several commissions too."

"He's only yanking my chain, babe," Kai says, pressing a kiss to Abby's temple.

"I know, but it's no harm to remind people." Abby is fiercely protective and supportive of Kai's passion, as she should be. He has really made a name for himself and he should be proud. His work is breathtaking. Truly exquisite, and he deserves every bit of his success.

"I saw that write-up on you in *The New York Times*," I tell Kaiden. "Impressive piece."

"Thanks. The guy was an asshole, and we butted heads a few times, so I wasn't expecting the article to be great," Kai admits. "Are you still painting furniture?" he asks.

"Just for pleasure, and only when I have free time." I had established a small side business for a couple of years after Charlie and I first got married, but I gave it up when the kids were small because I wanted to focus on our growing family.

"My wife has many talents," Charlie says, a smirk lifting the corners of his mouth.

Jackson makes a gagging sound while sticking two fingers in his mouth.

"My wife's pretty talented too," Kai says. "Just last night—"

Abby clamps her hand over her husband's mouth, muzzling him. "I'm shocked, Charlie," she adds. "It's usually Jackson who lowers the tone."

"I'll take that as a compliment." Jackson smirks, raising his beer to his lips as Vanessa rolls her eyes. "And I happen to be pretty talented myself," he adds, patting the top of her baby bump, his gaze brimming with pride.

"Oh boy." I shake my head, smiling at my husband. "You just had to go there, didn't you?"

Charlie presses his mouth to my ear. "I'm hoping for a display of those talents when we get home." He nips at my earlobe, and my core aches with longing.

Lillian arrived with her fiancé this evening, and they have taken the kids overnight. I could've kissed my sister-in-law when she offered. *I know she's dying to get married and start her own family, so who am I to deny her the opportunity for a trial run?*

I whisper into his ear. "Damn straight, stud. It's not often we have a kiddie-free house, and you can bet I intend to make the most of it." I slant him my most seductive look. "Why else do you think I brought the special toy chest with me?"

Charlie picks up my glass of wine, thrusting it at me. "Drink up. We're going home."

Fifteen minutes later, we're making hasty goodbyes as my husband hurries me away from the table. Our friends' catcalls and whistles follow us out the door.

"That was rude, Charlie."

He palms my ass through my dress as we walk along the path toward our vacation home. "Do I look like I care?" He reels me into his side. "I can't remember the last time I tied you up and fucked you six ways from Sunday. Shoot me if I'm enthusiastic."

I stop walking, pushing him into the railing that rims the front of the beach. I circle my arms around his neck, stretching up to kiss him. "Do I still do it for you, babe?"

"Don't ask stupid questions." He grabs onto my ass cheeks, pulling me into his erection. "You only have to glance at me, and I get hard."

I bark out a laugh, as I rock my hips into his. "Slight exaggeration, but I'll take it."

He thrusts his pelvis forward, and I see stars. "You'll take more than that."

I burst out in a fit of giggles, slowing to a halt when I spot the way he's looking at me. "What?"

He kisses me deeply, and I meet his lips with the same eagerness until we're making out like teenagers. "How did I get so lucky," he whispers when we finally break apart. His fingers sweep across my cheeks.

"How did I?" I agree, my voice dripping with lust. I pin him with a serious expression. "I love you, Charlie. Thank you for this wonderful life we share."

"I'm the one who should be thanking you."

An idea pops into my head. "Well, if you insist..." I can't contain my wicked smile.

"I know that look," he says, trailing his fingers up my bare thigh. "What naughty idea do you have in mind?"

I glance over his head, and he follows my line of sight, his lips kicking up.

"You haven't fucked me in a lifeguard tower before."

"I haven't," he agrees, grinning.

"Well, I think it's time you rectified that," I whisper, tugging on his hand and leading him down toward the beach.

"And we wonder where Jamie gets his ideas from," Charlie jokes, lifting me up.

I wrap my legs around his waist, and my arms go around his neck. "I'll claim credit," I tease, grazing my teeth along the side of his prickly jawline.

Charlie growls, picking up speed, as he heads for the white wooden structure.

He places my feet on the ground, and I untie my sandals and hitch my dress up so I can climb the ladder.

"My wife definitely has hidden talents," Charlie murmurs, watching me with an expression that is a mix of hunger and admiration as I move higher.

I look down at his handsome face, wiggling my fingers in a come hither gesture. "Get your sexy ass up here and let me show you."

He does, and I do, and as we lie tangled in each other's arms, staring up at the smattering of stars twinkling in the dark night sky, I offer up thanks for this gorgeous man sharing this life journey with me, and I know we have many more happy times to come.

The story continues in *Jackson*. Available now in ebook, paperback, alternate paperback and audiobook format.

The devil came to me in disguise. Too bad I didn't notice until it was far too late.

Vanessa

The devil doesn't always wear an evil mask.

Sometimes, he appears in the most beautiful form.

Like the super-hot bad boy with the dirty-blond hair and a wicked glint in his blue eyes who swept in out of nowhere, stealing all the air from my lungs.

I thought he was my savior.

But he's my ruination.

And he's just taken a machete to my heart.

Jackson

For years, my rage seethed under the surface. Hidden behind a cloudy haze of my poison of choice.

But now, the fog has cleared.

And I'm out for blood.

I will annihilate those responsible for taking my sister from me.

Except *he's* not here, so I go for the next best target.

The woman he abandoned.

Until it suited him to drag her into this messed-up elite world.

Sucks to be her.

Because when I'm done with Vanessa, she'll wish she was dead.

I didn't believe my fractured heart and broken soul could endure any more pain. Until Jared rocks up to the art gallery where I work, with his fiancée in tow, and I'm drowning again.

Seeing him brings everything to the surface, so I flee. Placing distance between us again, I'm determined to put him behind me once and for all.

Then he reappears at my door, begging me for another chance.

I know I should turn him away.

Try telling that to my heart.

This angsty, new adult romance is a FREE full-length ebook, exclusively available to newsletter subscribers.

Type this link into your browser to claim your free copy:

https://bit.ly/TITMHFBB

OR

Scan this code to claim your free copy:

About the Author

Siobhan Davis™ is a *USA Today, Wall Street Journal,* and Amazon Top 5 bestselling romance author. **Siobhan** writes emotionally intense stories with swoon-worthy romance, complex characters, and tons of unexpected plot twists and turns that will have you flipping the pages beyond bedtime! She has sold over 2 million books, and her titles are translated into several languages.

Prior to becoming a full-time writer, Siobhan forged a successful corporate career in human resource management.

She lives in the Garden County of Ireland with her husband and two sons.

You can connect with Siobhan in the following ways:

Website: www.siobhandavis.com
Facebook: AuthorSiobhanDavis
Instagram: @siobhandavisauthor
Tiktok: @siobhandavisauthor
Email: siobhan@siobhandavis.com

Books By Siobhan Davis

NEW ADULT ROMANCE

The One I Want Duet
Kennedy Boys Series
Rydeville Elite Series
All of Me Series
Forever Love Duet

NEW ADULT ROMANCE STAND-ALONES

Inseparable
Incognito
Still Falling for You
Holding on to Forever
Always Meant to Be
Tell It to My Heart

REVERSE HAREM

Sainthood Series
Dirty Crazy Bad Duet
Surviving Amber Springs (stand-alone)
Alinthia Series ^

DARK MAFIA ROMANCE

Mazzone Mafia Series
Vengeance of a Mafia Queen (stand-alone)
*The Accardi Twins**
*Taking What's Mine**

***

YA SCI-FI & PARANORMAL ROMANCE

Saven Series
True Calling Series ^

***

*Coming 2024
^Currently unpublished but will be republished in due course.

www.siobhandavis.com